THE BEST GOTHIC TALES AND GHOST STORIES

ARTHUR CONAN DOYLE

SANAGE
PUBLISHING HOUSE

Paperback: 978-936205037-3
Hardback: 978-936205740-2
eBook: 978-936205819-5

Sanage Publishing House LLP
Mumbai, India

sanagepublishing@gmail.com

Sir Arthur Ignatius Conan Doyle (22 May 1859 – 7 July 1930) was a British writer and medical doctor. Doyle began writing while studying at the University of Edinburgh Medical School, which he joined in 1876. Doyle graduated in 1881 and was employed as a surgeon on the steamer Mayumba on its voyage to the West African coast. He created the character Sherlock Holmes in 1887 for A Study in Scarlet, the first of four novels and fifty-six short stories about Holmes and Dr. Watson.

The Sherlock Holmes stories are generally considered milestones in the field of crime fiction.

Sherlock Holmes, the most well-known fictional detective, has been listed with Guinness World Records as the "most portrayed movie character" in history.

CONTENTS

LOT NO. 249

Of the dealings of Edward Bellingham with William Monkhouse Lee, and of the cause of the great terror of Abercrombie Smith, it may be that no absolute and final judgment will ever be delivered. It is true that we have the full and clear narrative of Smith himself, and such corroboration as he could look for from Thomas Styles the servant, from the Reverend Plumptree Peterson, Fellow of Old's, and from such other people as chanced to gain some passing glance at this or that incident in a singular chain of events. Yet, in the main, the story must rest upon Smith alone, and the most will think that it is more likely that one brain, however outwardly sane, has some subtle warp in its texture, some strange flaw in its workings, than that the path of Nature has been overstepped in open day in so famed a centre of learning and light as the University of Oxford. Yet when we think how narrow and how devious this path of Nature is, how dimly we can trace it, for all our lamps of science, and how from the darkness which girds it round great and terrible possibilities loom ever shadowly upwards, it is a bold and confident man who will put a limit to the strange by-paths into which the human spirit may wander.

In a certain wing of what we will call Old College in Oxford there is a corner turret of an exceeding great age. The heavy arch which spans the open door has bent downwards in the centre under the weight of its years, and the grey, lichen-blotched blocks of stone are, bound and knitted together with withes and strands of ivy, as though the old mother had set herself to brace them up against wind and weather. From the door a stone stair curves upward spirally, passing two landings, and terminating in a third one, its steps all shapeless and hollowed by the tread of so many generations of the seekers after knowledge. Life has flowed like water down this winding stair, and, waterlike, has left these smooth-worn grooves behind it. From the long-gowned, pedantic scholars of Plantagenet days down to the young bloods of a later age, how full and strong had been that tide of young English life. And what was left now of all those hopes, those strivings, those fiery energies, save here and there in some old-world churchyard a few scratches upon a stone, and perchance a handful of dust in a mouldering coffin? Yet here were the silent stair and the grey old wall, with bend and saltire and many another heraldic device still to be read upon its surface, like grotesque shadows thrown back from the days that had passed.

In the month of May, in the year 1884, three young men occupied the sets of rooms which opened on to the separate landings of the old stair. Each set consisted simply of a sitting-room and of a bedroom, while the two corresponding rooms upon the ground-floor were used, the one as a coal-cellar, and the other as the living-room of the servant, or gyp, Thomas Styles, whose duty it was to wait upon the three men above him. To right and to left was a line of lecture-rooms and of offices, so that the dwellers in the old turret enjoyed a certain seclusion, which made the chambers popular among the more studious undergraduates. Such were the three who occupied them now— Abercrombie Smith above, Edward Bellingham beneath him, and William Monkhouse Lee upon the lowest storey.

It was ten o'clock on a bright spring night, and Abercrombie Smith lay back in his arm-chair, his feet upon the fender, and his briar-root pipe between his lips. In a similar chair, and equally at his ease, there lounged on the other side of the fireplace his old school friend Jephro Hastie. Both men were in flannels, for they had spent their evening upon the river, but apart from their dress no one could look at their hard-cut, alert faces without seeing that they were open-air men— men whose minds and tastes turned naturally to all that was manly and robust. Hastie, indeed, was stroke of his college boat, and Smith was an even better oar, but a coming examination had already cast its shadow over him and held him to his work, save for the few hours a week which health demanded. A litter of medical books upon the table, with scattered bones, models and anatomical plates, pointed to the extent as well as the nature of his studies, while a couple of single-sticks and a set of boxing-gloves above the mantelpiece hinted at the means by which, with Hastie's help, he might take his exercise in its most compressed and least distant form. They knew each other very well—so well that they could sit now in that soothing silence which is the very highest development of companionship.

"Have some whisky," said Abercrombie Smith at last between two cloudbursts. "Scotch in the jug and Irish in the bottle."

"No, thanks. I'm in for the sculls. I don't liquor when I'm training. How about you?"

"I'm reading hard. I think it best to leave it alone."

Hastie nodded, and they relapsed into a contented silence.

"By-the-way, Smith," asked Hastie, presently, "have you made the acquaintance of either of the fellows on your stair yet?"

"Just a nod when we pass. Nothing more."

"Hum! I should be inclined to let it stand at that. I know something of them both. Not much, but as much as I want. I don't think I should take them to my bosom if I were you. Not that there's much amiss with Monkhouse Lee."

"Meaning the thin one?"

"Precisely. He is a gentlemanly little fellow. I don't think there is any vice in him. But then you can't know him without knowing Bellingham."

"Meaning the fat one?"

"Yes, the fat one. And he's a man whom I, for one, would rather not know."

Abercrombie Smith raised his eyebrows and glanced across at his companion.

"What's up, then?" he asked. "Drink? Cards? Cad? You used not to be censorious."

"Ah! you evidently don't know the man, or you wouldn't ask. There's something damnable about him—something reptilian. My gorge always rises at him. I should put him down as a man with secret vices—an evil liver. He's no fool, though. They say that he is one of the best men in his line that they have ever had in the college."

"Medicine or classics?"

"Eastern languages. He's a demon at them. Chillingworth met him somewhere above the second cataract last long, and he told me that he just prattled to the Arabs as if he had been born and nursed and weaned among them. He talked Coptic to the Copts, and Hebrew to the Jews, and Arabic to the Bedouins, and they were all ready to kiss the hem of his frock-coat. There are some old hermit Johnnies up in those parts who sit on rocks and scowl and spit at the casual stranger. Well, when they saw this chap Bellingham, before he had said five words they just lay down on their bellies and wriggled. Chillingworth said that he never saw anything like it. Bellingham seemed to take it as his right, too, and strutted about among them and talked down to them like a Dutch uncle. Pretty good for an undergrad. of Old's, wasn't it?"

"Why do you say you can't know Lee without knowing Bellingham?"

"Because Bellingham is engaged to his sister Eveline. Such a bright little girl, Smith! I know the whole family well. It's disgusting to see that brute with her. A toad and a dove, that's what they always remind me of."

Abercrombie Smith grinned and knocked his ashes out against the side of the grate.

"You show every card in your hand, old chap," said he. "What a prejudiced, green-eyed, evil-thinking old man it is! You have really nothing against the fellow except that."

"Well, I've known her ever since she was as long as that cherry-wood pipe, and I don't like to see her taking risks. And it is a risk. He looks beastly. And he has a beastly temper, a venomous temper. You remember his row with Long Norton?"

"No; you always forget that I am a freshman."

"Ah, it was last winter. Of course. Well, you know the towpath along by the river. There were several fellows going along it, Bellingham in front, when they came on an old market-woman coming the other way. It had been raining—you know what those fields are like when it has rained—and the path ran between the river and a great puddle that was nearly as broad. Well, what does this swine do but keep the path, and push the old girl into the mud, where she and her marketings came to terrible grief. It was a blackguard thing to do, and Long Norton, who is as gentle a fellow as ever stepped, told him what he thought of it. One word led to another, and it ended in Norton laying his stick across the fellow's shoulders. There was the deuce of a fuss about it, and it's a treat to see the way in which Bellingham looks at Norton when they meet now. By Jove, Smith, it's nearly eleven o'clock!"

"No hurry. Light your pipe again."

"Not I. I'm supposed to be in training. Here I've been sitting gossiping when I ought to have been safely tucked up. I'll borrow your skull, if you can share it. Williams has had mine for a month. I'll take the little bones of your ear, too, if you are sure you won't need them. Thanks very much. Never mind a bag, I can carry them very well under my arm. Good-night, my son, and take my tip as to your neighbour."

When Hastie, bearing his anatomical plunder, had clattered off down the winding stair, Abercrombie Smith hurled his pipe into the wastepaper basket, and drawing his chair nearer to the lamp, plunged into a formidable, green-covered volume, adorned with great colored maps of that strange internal kingdom of which we are the hapless and helpless monarchs. Though a freshman at Oxford, the student was not so in medicine, for he had worked for four years at Glasgow and at Berlin, and this coming examination would place him finally as a member of his profession. With his firm mouth, broad forehead, and clear-cut, somewhat hard-featured face, he was a man who, if he had no brilliant talent, was yet so dogged, so patient, and so strong that he might in the end overtop a more showy genius. A man who can hold his own among Scotchmen and North Germans is not a man to be easily set back. Smith had left a name at Glasgow and at Berlin, and he was bent now upon doing as much at Oxford, if hard work and devotion could accomplish it.

He had sat reading for about an hour, and the hands of the noisy carriage clock upon the side table were rapidly closing together upon the twelve, when a sudden sound fell upon the student's ear—a sharp, rather shrill sound, like the hissing intake of a man's breath who gasps under some strong emotion. Smith laid down his book and slanted his ear to listen. There was no one on either side or above him, so that the interruption came certainly from the neighbour beneath—the same neighbour of whom Hastie had given so unsavoury an account. Smith knew him only as a flabby, pale-faced man of silent and studious habits, a man, whose lamp threw a golden bar from the old turret even after he had extinguished his own. This community in lateness had formed a certain silent bond between them. It was soothing to Smith when the hours stole on towards dawning to feel that there was another so close who set as small a value upon his sleep as he did. Even now, as his thoughts turned towards him, Smith's feelings were kindly. Hastie was a good fellow, but he was rough, strong-fibred, with no imagination or sympathy. He could not tolerate departures from what he looked upon as the model type of manliness. If a man could not be measured by a public-school standard, then he was beyond the pale with Hastie. Like so many who are themselves robust, he was apt to confuse the constitution with the character, to ascribe to want of principle what was really a want of circulation. Smith, with his stronger mind, knew his friend's habit, and made allowance for it now as his thoughts turned towards the man beneath him.

There was no return of the singular sound, and Smith was about to turn to his work once more, when suddenly there broke out in the silence of the night a hoarse cry, a positive scream—the call of a man who is moved and shaken beyond all control. Smith sprang out of his chair and dropped his book. He was a man of fairly firm fibre but there was something in this sudden, uncontrollable shriek of horror which chilled his blood and pringled in his skin. Coming in such a place and at such an hour, it brought a thousand fantastic possibilities into his head. Should he rush down, or was it better to wait? He had all the national hatred of making a scene, and he knew so little of his neighbour that he would not lightly intrude upon his affairs. For a moment he stood in doubt and even as he balanced the matter there was a quick rattle of footsteps upon the stairs, and young Monkhouse Lee, half dressed and as white as ashes, burst into his room.

"Come down!" he gasped. "Bellingham's ill."

Abercrombie Smith followed him closely downstairs into the sitting-room which was beneath his own, and intent as he was upon the matter in hand, he could not but take an amazed glance around him as he crossed the threshold. It was such a chamber as he had never seen before—a museum rather than a study. Walls and ceiling were thickly covered with a thousand strange relics from Egypt and the East. Tall, angular figures bearing burdens or weapons stalked in an uncouth frieze round the apartments. Above were bull-headed, stork-headed, cat-headed, owl-headed statues, with viper-crowned, almond-eyed monarchs, and strange, beetle-like deities cut out of the blue Egyptian lapis lazuli. Horus and Isis and Osiris peeped down from every niche and shelf, while across the ceiling a true son of Old Nile, a great, hanging-jawed crocodile, was slung in a double noose.

In the centre of this singular chamber was a large, square table, littered with papers, bottles, and the dried leaves of some graceful, palm-like plant. These varied objects had all been heaped together in order to make room for a mummy case, which had been conveyed from the wall, as was evident from the gap there, and laid across the front of the table. The mummy itself, a horrid, black, withered thing, like a charred head on a gnarled bush, was lying half out of the case, with its clawlike hand and bony forearm resting upon the table. Propped up against the sarcophagus was an old yellow scroll of papyrus, and in front of it, in a wooden armchair, sat the owner of the room, his head thrown back, his widely-opened eyes directed in a horrified stare to the crocodile above him, and his blue, thick lips puffing loudly with every expiration.

"My God! he's dying!" cried Monkhouse Lee distractedly.

He was a slim, handsome young fellow, olive-skinned and dark-eyed, of a Spanish rather than of an English type, with a Celtic intensity of manner which contrasted with the Saxon phlegm of Abercombie Smith.

"Only a faint, I think," said the medical student. "Just give me a hand with him. You take his feet. Now on to the sofa. Can you kick all those little wooden devils off? What a litter it is! Now he will be all right if we undo his collar and give him some water. What has he been up to at all?"

"I don't know. I heard him cry out. I ran up. I know him pretty well, you know. It is very good of you to come down."

"His heart is going like a pair of castanets," said Smith, laying his hand on the breast of the unconscious man. "He seems to me to be frightened all to pieces. Chuck the water over him! What a face he has got on him!"

It was indeed a strange and most repellent face, for colour and outline were equally unnatural. It was white, not with the ordinary pallor of fear but with an absolutely bloodless white, like the underside of a sole. He was very fat but gave the impression of having at some time been considerably fatter, for his skin hung loosely increases and folds and was shot with a meshwork of wrinkles. Short, stubbly brown hair bristled up from his scalp, with a pair of thick, wrinkled ears protruding on either side. His light grey eyes were still open, the pupils dilated and the balls projecting in a fixed and horrid stare. It seemed to Smith as he looked down upon him that he had never seen nature's danger signals flying so plainly upon a man's countenance, and his thoughts turned more seriously to the warning which Hastie had given him an hour before.

"What the deuce can have frightened him so?" he asked.

"It's the mummy."

"The mummy? How, then?"

"I don't know. It's beastly and morbid. I wish he would drop it. It's the second fright he has given me. It was the same last winter. I found him just like this, with that horrid thing in front of him."

"What does he want with the mummy, then?"

"Oh, he's a crank, you know. It's his hobby. He knows more about these things than any man in England. But I wish he wouldn't! Ah, he's beginning to come to."

A faint tinge of colour had begun to steal back into Bellingham's ghastly cheeks, and his eyelids shivered like a sail after a calm. He clasped and unclasped his hands, drew a long, thin breath between his teeth, and suddenly jerking up his head, threw a glance of recognition around him. As his eyes fell upon the mummy, he sprang off the sofa, seized the roll of papyrus, thrust it into a drawer, turned the key, and then staggered back on to the sofa.

"What's up?" he asked. "What do you chaps want?"

"You've been shrieking out and making no end of a fuss," said Monkhouse Lee. "If our neighbour here from above hadn't come down, I'm sure I don't know what I should have done with you."

"Ah, it's Abercrombie Smith," said Bellingham, glancing up at him. "How very good of you to come in! What a fool I am! Oh, my God, what a fool I am!"

He sunk his head on to his hands and burst into peal after peal of hysterical laughter.

"Look here! Drop it!" cried Smith, shaking him roughly by the shoulder.

"Your nerves are all in a jangle. You must drop these little midnight games with mummies, or you'll be going off your chump. You're all on wires now."

"I wonder," said Bellingham, "whether you would be as cool as I am if you had seen———"

"What then?"

"Oh, nothing. I meant that I wonder if you could sit up at night with a mummy without trying your nerves. I have no doubt that you are quite right. I dare say that I have been taking it out of myself too much lately. But I am all right now. Please don't go, though. Just wait for a few minutes until I am quite myself."

"The room is very close," remarked Lee, throwing open the window and letting in the cool night air.

"It's balsamic resin," said Bellingham. He lifted up one of the dried palmate leaves from the table and frizzled it over the chimney of the lamp. It broke away into heavy smoke wreaths, and a pungent, biting odour filled the chamber. "It's the sacred plant—the plant of the priests," he remarked. "Do you know anything of Eastern languages, Smith?"

"Nothing at all. Not a word."

The answer seemed to lift a weight from the Egyptologist's mind.

"By-the-way," he continued, "how long was it from the time that you ran down, until I came to my senses?"

"Not long. Some four or five minutes."

"I thought it could not be very long," said he, drawing a long breath. "But what a strange thing unconsciousness is! There is no measurement to it. I could not tell from my own sensations if it were seconds or weeks. Now that gentleman on the table was packed up in the days of the eleventh dynasty, some forty centuries ago, and yet if he could find his tongue he would tell us that this lapse of time has been but a closing of the eyes and a reopening of them. He is a singularly fine mummy, Smith."

Smith stepped over to the table and looked down with a professional eye at the black and twisted form in front of him. The features, though horribly discoloured, were perfect, and two little nut-like eyes still lurked in the depths of the black, hollow sockets. The blotched skin was drawn tightly from bone to bone, and a tangled wrap of black coarse hair fell over the ears. Two thin teeth, like those of a rat, overlay the shrivelled lower lip. In its crouching position, with bent joints and craned head, there was a suggestion of energy about the horrid thing which made Smith's gorge rise. The gaunt ribs, with their parchment-like covering, were exposed, and the sunken, leaden-hued abdomen, with the long slit where the embalmer had left his mark; but the lower limbs were wrapt round with coarse yellow bandages. A number of little clove-like pieces of myrrh and of cassia were sprinkled over the body and lay scattered on the inside of the case.

"I don't know his name," said Bellingham, passing his hand over the shrivelled head. "You see the outer sarcophagus with the inscriptions is missing. Lot 249 is all the title he has now. You see it printed on his case. That was his number in the auction at which I picked him up."

"He has been a very pretty sort of fellow in his day," remarked Abercrombie Smith.

"He has been a giant. His mummy is six feet seven in length, and that would be a giant over there, for they were never a very robust race. Feel these great knotted bones, too. He would be a nasty fellow to tackle."

"Perhaps these very hands helped to build the stones into the pyramids," suggested Monkhouse Lee, looking down with disgust in his eyes at the crooked, unclean talons.

"No fear. This fellow has been pickled in natron and looked after in the most approved style. They did not serve hodsmen in that fashion. Salt or bitumen was enough for them. It has been calculated that this sort of thing cost about seven hundred and thirty pounds in our money. Our friend was a noble at the least. What do you make of that small inscription near his feet, Smith?"

"I told you that I know no Eastern tongue."

"Ah, so you did. It is the name of the embalmer, I take it. A very conscientious worker he must have been. I wonder how many modern works will survive four thousand years?"

He kept on speaking lightly and rapidly, but it was evident to Abercrombie Smith that he was still palpitating with fear. His hands shook, his lower lip trembled, and look where he would, his eye always came sliding round to his gruesome companion. Through all his fear, however, there was a suspicion of triumph in his tone and manner. His eye shone, and his footstep, as he paced the room, was brisk and jaunty. He gave the impression of a man who has gone through an ordeal, the marks of which he still bears upon him, but which has helped him to his end.

"You're not going yet?" he cried, as Smith rose from the sofa.

At the prospect of solitude, his fears seemed to crowd back upon him, and he stretched out a hand to detain him.

"Yes, I must go. I have my work to do. You are all right now. I think that with your nervous system you should take up some less morbid study."

"Oh, I am not nervous as a rule; and I have unwrapped mummies before."

"You fainted last time," observed Monkhouse Lee.

"Ah, yes, so I did. Well, I must have a nerve tonic or a course of electricity. You are not going, Lee?"

"I'll do whatever you wish, Ned."

"Then I'll come down with you and have a shake-down on your sofa. Good-night, Smith. I am so sorry to have disturbed you with my foolishness."

They shook hands, and as the medical student stumbled up the spiral and irregular stair he heard a key turn in a door, and the steps of his two new acquaintances as they descended to the lower floor.

In this strange way began the acquaintance between Edward Bellingham and Abercrombie Smith, an acquaintance which the latter, at least, had no desire to push further. Bellingham, however, appeared to have taken a fancy to his rough-spoken neighbour, and made his advances in such a way that he could hardly be repulsed without absolute brutality. Twice he called to thank Smith for his assistance, and many times afterwards he looked in with books, papers, and such other civilities as two bachelor neighbours can offer each other. He was, as Smith soon found, a man of wide reading, with catholic tastes and an extraordinary memory. His manner, too, was so pleasing and suave that one came, after a time, to overlook his repellent appearance. For a jaded and wearied man, he was no unpleasant companion and Smith found himself, after a time, looking forward to his visits, and even returning them.

Clever as he undoubtedly was, however, the medical student seemed to detect a dash of insanity in the man. He broke out at times into a high, inflated style of talk which was in contrast with the simplicity of his life.

"It is a wonderful thing," he cried, "to feel that one can command powers of good and of evil—a ministering angel or a demon of vengeance." And again, of Monkhouse Lee, he said,—"Lee is a good fellow, an honest fellow, but he is without strength or ambition. He would not make a fit partner for a man with a great enterprise. He would not make a fit partner for me."

At such hints and innuendoes stolid Smith, puffing solemnly at his pipe, would simply raise his eyebrows and shake his head, with little interjections of medical wisdom as to earlier hours and fresher air.

One habit Bellingham had developed of late which Smith knew to be a frequent herald of a weakening mind. He appeared to be forever talking to himself. At late hours of the night, when there could be no visitor with him, Smith could still hear his voice beneath him in a low, muffled monologue, sunk almost to a whisper, and yet very audible in the silence. This solitary babbling annoyed and distracted the student, so that he spoke more than once to his neighbour about it. Bellingham, however, flushed up at the charge, and denied curtly that he had uttered a sound; indeed, he showed more annoyance over the matter than the occasion seemed to demand.

Had Abercrombie Smith had any doubt as to his own ears he had not to go far to find corroboration. Tom Styles, the little wrinkled man-servant who had attended to the wants of the lodgers in the turret for a longer time than any man's memory could carry him, was sorely put to it over the same matter.

"If you please, sir," said he, as he tidied down the top chamber one morning, "do you think Mr. Bellingham is all right, sir?"

"All right, Styles?"

"Yes sir. Right in his head, sir."

"Why should he not be, then?"

"Well, I don't know, sir. His habits has changed of late. He's not the same man he used to be, though I make free to say that he was never quite one of my gentlemen, like Mr. Hastie or yourself, sir. He's took to talkin' to himself something awful. I wonder it don't disturb you. I don't know what to make of him, sir."

"I don't know what business it is of yours, Styles."

"Well, I takes an interest, Mr. Smith. It may be forward of me, but I can't help it. I feel sometimes as if I was mother and father to my young gentlemen. It all falls on me when things go wrong, and the relations come. But Mr. Bellingham, sir. I want to know what it is that walks about his room sometimes when he's out and when the door's locked on the outside."

"Eh! you're talking nonsense, Styles."

"Maybe so, sir; but I heard it more'n once with my own ears."

"Rubbish, Styles."

"Very good, sir. You'll ring the bell if you want me."

Abercrombie Smith gave little heed to the gossip of the old man-servant, but a small incident occurred a few days later which left an unpleasant effect upon his mind and brought the words of Styles forcibly to his memory.

Bellingham had come up to see him late one night and was entertaining him with an interesting account of the rock tombs of Beni Hassan in Upper Egypt, when Smith, whose hearing was remarkably acute, distinctly heard the sound of a door opening on the landing below.

"There's some fellow gone in or out of your room," he remarked.

Bellingham sprang up and stood helpless for a moment, with the expression of a man who is half incredulous and half afraid.

"I surely locked it. I am almost positive that I locked it," he stammered. "No one could have opened it."

"Why, I hear someone coming up the steps now," said Smith.

Bellingham rushed out through the door, slammed it loudly behind him, and hurried down the stairs. About half-way down Smith heard him stop, and thought he caught the sound of whispering. A moment later the door beneath him shut, a key creaked in a lock, and Bellingham, with beads of moisture upon his pale face, ascended the stairs once more, and re-entered the room.

"It's all right," he said, throwing himself down in a chair. "It was that fool of a dog. He had pushed the door open. I don't know how I came to forget to lock it."

"I didn't know you kept a dog," said Smith, looking very thoughtfully at the disturbed face of his companion.

"Yes, I haven't had him long. I must get rid of him. He's a great nuisance."

"He must be, if you find it so hard to shut him up. I should have thought that shutting the door would have been enough, without locking it."

"I want to prevent old Styles from letting him out. He's of some value, you know, and it would be awkward to lose him."

"I am a bit of a dog-fancier myself," said Smith, still gazing hard at his companion from the corner of his eyes. "Perhaps you'll let me have a look at it."

"Certainly. But I am afraid it cannot be tonight; I have an appointment. Is that clock right? Then I am a quarter of an hour late already. You'll excuse me, I am sure."

He picked up his cap and hurried from the room. In spite of his appointment, Smith heard him re-enter his own chamber and lock his door upon the inside.

This interview left a disagreeable impression upon the medical student's mind. Bellingham had lied to him and lied so clumsily that it looked as if he had desperate reasons for concealing the truth. Smith knew that his neighbour had no dog. He knew, also, that the step which he had heard upon the stairs was not the step of an animal. But if it were not, then what could it be? There was old Styles's statement about the something which used to pace the room at times when the owner was absent. Could it be a woman? Smith rather inclined to the view. If so, it would mean disgrace and expulsion to Bellingham if it were discovered by the authorities, so that his anxiety and falsehoods might be accounted for. And yet it was inconceivable that an undergraduate could keep a woman in his rooms without being instantly detected. Be the explanation what it might, there was something ugly about it, and Smith determined, as he turned to his books, to discourage all further attempts at intimacy on the part of his soft-spoken and ill-favoured neighbour.

But his work was destined to interruption that night. He had hardly caught tip the broken threads when a firm, heavy footfall came three steps at a time from below, and Hastie, in blazer and flannels, burst into the room.

"Still at it!" said he, plumping down into his wonted arm-chair. "What a chap you are to stew! I believe an earthquake might come and knock Oxford into a cocked hat, and you would sit perfectly placid with your books among the rains. However, I won't bore you long. Three whiffs of baccy, and I am off."

"What's the news, then?" asked Smith, cramming a plug of bird's-eye into his briar with his forefinger.

"Nothing very much. Wilson made 70 for the freshmen against the eleven. They say that they will play him instead of Buddicomb, for Buddicomb is clean off colour. He used to be able to bowl a little, but it's nothing but half-vollies and long hops now."

"Medium right," suggested Smith, with the intense gravity which comes upon a 'varsity man when he speaks of athletics.

"Inclining to fast, with a work from leg. Comes with the arm about three inches or so. He used to be nasty on a wet wicket. Oh, by-the-way, have you heard about Long Norton?"

"What's that?"

"He's been attacked."

"Attacked?"

"Yes, just as he was turning out of the High Street, and within a hundred yards of the gate of Old's."

"But who———"

"Ah, that's the rub! If you said 'what,' you would be more grammatical. Norton swears that it was not human, and, indeed, from the scratches on his throat, I should be inclined to agree with him."

"What, then? Have we come down to spooks?"

Abercrombie Smith puffed his scientific contempt.

"Well, no; I don't think that is quite the idea, either. I am inclined to think that if any showman has lost a great ape lately, and the brute is in these parts, a jury would find a true bill against it. Norton passes that way every night, you know, about the same hour. There's a tree that hangs low over the path—the big elm from Rainy's garden. Norton thinks the thing dropped on him out of the tree. Anyhow, he was nearly strangled by two arms, which, he says, were as strong and as thin as steel bands. He saw nothing; only those beastly arms that tightened and tightened on him. He yelled his head nearly off, and a couple of chaps came running, and the thing went over the wall like a cat. He never got a fair sight of it the whole time. It gave Norton a shake up, I can tell you. I tell him it has been as good as a change at the sea-side for him."

"A garrotter, most likely," said Smith.

"Very possibly. Norton says not; but we don't mind what he says. The garrotter had long nails, and was pretty smart at swinging himself over walls. By-the-way, your beautiful neighbour would be pleased if he heard about it. He had a grudge against Norton, and he's not a man, from what I know of him, to forget his little debts. But hallo, old chap, what have you got in your noddle?"

"Nothing," Smith answered curtly.

He had started in his chair, and the look had flashed over his face which comes upon a man who is struck suddenly by some unpleasant idea.

"You looked as if something I had said had taken you on the raw. By-the-way, you have made the acquaintance of Master B. since I looked in last, have you not? Young Monkhouse Lee told me something to that effect."

"Yes; I know him slightly. He has been up here once or twice."

"Well, you're big enough and ugly enough to take care of yourself. He's not what I should call exactly a healthy sort of Johnny, though, no doubt, he's very clever, and all that. But you'll soon find out for yourself. Lee is all right; he's a very decent little fellow. Well, so long, old chap! I row Mullins for the Vice-Chancellor's pot on Wednesday week, so mind you come down, in case I don't see you before."

Bovine Smith laid down his pipe and turned stolidly to his books once more. But with all the will in the world, he found it very hard to keep his mind upon his work. It would slip away to brood upon the man beneath him, and upon the little mystery which hung round his chambers. Then his thoughts turned to this singular attack of which Hastie had spoken, and to the grudge which Bellingham was said to owe the object of it. The two ideas would persist in rising together in his mind, as though there were some close and intimate connection between them. And yet the suspicion was so dim and vague that it could not be put down in words.

"Confound the chap!" cried Smith, as he shied his book on pathology across the room. "He has spoiled my night's reading, and that's reason enough, if there were no other, why I should steer clear of him in the future."

For ten days the medical student confined himself so closely to his studies that he neither saw nor heard anything of either of the men beneath him. At the hours when Bellingham had been accustomed to visit him, he took care to sport his oak, and though he more than once heard a knocking at his outer door, he resolutely refused to answer it. One afternoon, however, he was descending the stairs when, just as he was passing it, Bellingham's door flew open, and young Monkhouse

Lee came out with his eyes sparkling and a dark flush of anger upon his olive cheeks. Close at his heels followed Bellingham, his fat, unhealthy face all quivering with malignant passion.

"You fool!" he hissed. "You'll be sorry."

"Very likely," cried the other. "Mind what I say. It's off! I won't hear of it!"

"You've promised, anyhow."

"Oh, I'll keep that! I won't speak. But I'd rather little Eva was in her grave. Once for all, it's off. She'll do what I say. We don't want to see you again."

So much Smith could not avoid hearing, but he hurried on, for he had no wish to be involved in their dispute. There had been a serious breach between them, that was clear enough, and Lee was going to cause the engagement with his sister to be broken off. Smith thought of Hastie's comparison of the toad and the dove and was glad to think that the matter was at an end. Bellingham's face when he was in a passion was not pleasant to look upon. He was not a man to whom an innocent girl could be trusted for life. As he walked, Smith wondered languidly what could have caused the quarrel, and what the promise might be which Bellingham had been so anxious that Monkhouse Lee should keep.

It was the day of the sculling match between Hastie and Mullins, and a stream of men were making their way down to the banks of the Isis. A May sun was shining brightly, and the yellow path was barred with the black shadows of the tall elm-trees. On either side the grey colleges lay back from the road, the hoary old mothers of minds looking out from their high, mullioned windows at the tide of young life which swept so merrily past them. Black-clad tutors, prim officials, pale reading men, brown-faced, straw-hatted young athletes in white sweaters or many-coloured blazers, all were hurrying towards the blue winding river which curves through the Oxford meadows.

Abercrombie Smith, with the intuition of an old oarsman, chose his position at the point where he knew that the struggle, if there were a struggle, would come. Far off he heard the hum which announced the start, the gathering roar of the approach, the thunder of running feet, and the shouts of the men in the boats beneath him. A spray of half-clad, deep-breathing runners shot past him, and craning over their shoulders, he saw Hastie pulling a steady thirty-six, while his opponent, with a jerky forty, was a good boat's length behind him. Smith gave a cheer for his friend, and pulling out his watch, was starting off again for his chambers, when he felt a touch upon his shoulder, and found that young Monkhouse Lee was beside him.

"I saw you there," he said, in a timid, deprecating way. "I wanted to speak to you, if you could spare me a half-hour. This cottage is mine. I share it with Harrington of King's. Come in and have a cup of tea."

"I must be back presently," said Smith. "I am hard on the grind at present. But I'll come in for a few minutes with pleasure. I wouldn't have come out only Hastie is a friend of mine."

"So he is of mine. Hasn't he a beautiful style? Mullins wasn't in it. But come into the cottage. It's a little den of a place, but it is pleasant to work in during the summer months."

It was a small, square, white building, with green doors and shutters, and a rustic trellis-work porch, standing back some fifty yards from the river's bank. Inside, the main room was roughly fitted up as a study—deal table, unpainted shelves with books, and a few cheap oleographs upon the wall. A kettle sang upon a spirit-stove, and there were tea things upon a tray on the table.

"Try that chair and have a cigarette," said Lee. "Let me pour you out a cup of tea. It's so good of you to come in, for I know that your time is a good deal taken up. I wanted to say to you that, if I were you, I should change my rooms at once."

"Eh?"

Smith sat staring with a lighted match in one hand and his unlit cigarette in the other.

"Yes; it must seem very extraordinary, and the worst of it is that I cannot give my reasons, for I am under a solemn promise—a very solemn promise. But I may go so far as to say that I don't think Bellingham is a very safe man to live near. I intend to camp out here as much as I can for a time."

"Not safe! What do you mean?"

"Ah, that's what I mustn't say. But do take my advice and move your rooms. We had a grand row today. You must have heard us, for you came down the stairs."

"I saw that you had fallen out."

"He's a horrible chap, Smith. That is the only word for him. I have had doubts about him ever since that night when he fainted—you remember, when you came down. I taxed him today, and he told me things that made my hair rise and wanted me to stand in with him. I'm not strait-laced, but I am a clergyman's son, you know, and I think there are some things which are quite beyond the pale. I only thank God that I found him out before it was too late, for he was to have married into my family."

"This is all very fine, Lee," said Abercrombie Smith curtly. "But either you are saying a great deal too much or a great deal too little."

"I give you a warning."

"If there is real reason for warning, no promise can bind you. If I see a rascal about to blow a place up with dynamite no pledge will stand in my way of preventing him."

"Ah, but I cannot prevent him, and I can do nothing but warn you."

"Without saying what you warn me against."

"Against Bellingham."

"But that is childish. Why should I fear him, or any man?"

"I can't tell you. I can only entreat you to change your rooms. You are in danger where you are. I don't even say that Bellingham would wish to injure you. But it might happen, for he is a dangerous neighbour just now."

"Perhaps I know more than you think," said Smith, looking keenly at the young man's boyish, earnest face. "Suppose I tell you that someone else shares Bellingham's rooms."

Monkhouse Lee sprang from his chair in uncontrollable excitement.

"You know, then?" he gasped.

"A woman."

Lee dropped back again with a groan.

"My lips are sealed," he said. "I must not speak."

"Well, anyhow," said Smith, rising, "it is not likely that I should allow myself to be frightened out of rooms which suit me very nicely. It would be a little too feeble for me to move out all my goods and chattels because you say that Bellingham might in some unexplained way do me an injury. I think that I'll just take my chance, and stay where I am, and as I see that it's nearly five o'clock, I must ask you to excuse me."

He bade the young student adieu in a few curt words and made his way homeward through the sweet spring evening feeling half-ruffled, half-amused, as any other strong, unimaginative man might who has been menaced by a vague and shadowy danger.

There was one little indulgence which Abercrombie Smith always allowed himself, however closely his work might press upon him. Twice a week, on the Tuesday and the Friday, it was his invariable custom to walk over to Farlingford, the residence of Dr. Plumptree Peterson, situated about a mile and a half out of Oxford. Peterson had been a close friend of Smith's elder brother Francis, and as he was a bachelor, fairly well-to-do, with a good cellar and a better library, his house was a pleasant goal for a man who was in need of a brisk walk. Twice a week, then, the medical student would swing out there along the dark country roads, and spend a pleasant hour in Peterson's comfortable study, discussing, over a glass of old port, the gossip of the 'varsity or the latest developments of medicine or of surgery.

On the day which followed his interview with Monkhouse Lee, Smith shut up his books at a quarter past eight, the hour when he usually started for his friend's house. As he was leaving his room, however, his eyes chanced to fall upon one of the books which Bellingham had lent him, and his conscience pricked him for not having returned it. However repellent the man might be, he should not be treated with discourtesy. Taking the book, he walked downstairs and knocked at his neighbour's door. There was no answer; but on turning the handle he found that it was unlocked. Pleased at the thought of avoiding an interview, he stepped inside and placed the book with his card upon the table.

The lamp was turned half down, but Smith could see the details of the room plainly enough. It was all much as he had seen it before—the frieze, the animal-headed gods, the banging crocodile, and the table littered over with papers and dried leaves. The mummy case stood upright against the wall, but the mummy itself was missing. There was no sign of any second occupant of the room, and he felt as he withdrew that he had probably done Bellingham an injustice. Had he a guilty secret to preserve, he would hardly leave his door open so that all the world might enter.

The spiral stair was as black as pitch, and Smith was slowly making his way down its irregular steps, when he was suddenly conscious that something had passed him in the darkness. There was a faint sound, a whiff of air, a light brushing past his elbow, but so slight that he could scarcely be certain of it. He stopped and listened, but the wind was rustling among the ivy outside, and he could hear nothing else.

"Is that you, Styles?" he shouted.

There was no answer, and all was still behind him. It must have been a sudden gust of air, for there were crannies and cracks in the old turret. And yet he could almost have sworn that he heard a footfall by his very side. He had emerged into the quadrangle, still turning the matter over in his head, when a man came running swiftly across the smooth-cropped lawn.

"Is that you, Smith?"

"Hullo, Hastie!"

"For God's sake come at once! Young Lee is drowned! Here's Harrington of King's with the news. The doctor is out. You'll do but come along at once. There may be life in him."

"Have you brandy?"

"No."

"I'll bring some. There's a flask on my table."

Smith bounded up the stairs, taking three at a time, seized the flask, and was rushing down with it, when, as he passed Bellingham's room, his eyes fell upon something which left him gasping and staring upon the landing.

The door, which he had closed behind him, was now open, and right in front of him, with the lamp-light shining upon it, was the mummy case. Three minutes ago, it had been empty. He could swear to that. Now it framed the lank body of its horrible occupant, who stood, grim and stark, with his black shrivelled face towards the door. The form was lifeless and inert, but it seemed to Smith as he gazed that there still lingered a lurid spark of vitality, some faint sign of consciousness in the little eyes which lurked in the depths of the hollow sockets. So astounded and shaken was he that he had forgotten his errand, and was still staring at the lean, sunken figure when the voice of his friend below recalled him to himself.

"Come on, Smith!" he shouted. "It's life and death, you know. Hurry up! Now, then," he added, as the medical student reappeared, "let us do a sprint. It is well under a mile, and we should do it in five minutes. A human life is better worth running for than a pot."

Neck and neck they dashed through the darkness, and did not pull up until, panting and spent, they had reached the little cottage by the river. Young Lee, limp and dripping like a broken water-plant, was stretched upon the sofa, the green scum of the river upon his black hair, and a fringe of white foam upon his leaden-hued lips. Beside him knelt his fellow-student Harrington, endeavouring to chafe some warmth back into his rigid limbs.

"I think there's life in him," said Smith, with his hand to the lad's side. "Put your watch glass to his lips. Yes, there's dimming on it. You take one arm, Hastie. Now work it as I do, and we'll soon pull him round."

For ten minutes they worked in silence, inflating and depressing the chest of the unconscious man. At the end of that time a shiver ran through his body, his lips trembled, and he opened his eyes. The three students burst out into an irrepressible cheer.

"Wake up, old chap. You've frightened us quite enough."

"Have some brandy. Take a sip from the flask."

"He's all right now," said his companion Harrington. "Heavens, what a fright I got! I was reading here, and he had gone for a stroll as far as the river, when I heard a scream and a splash. Out I ran, and by the time that I could find him and fish him out, all life seemed to have gone. Then Simpson couldn't get a doctor, for he has a game-leg, and I had to run, and I don't know what I'd have done without you fellows. That's right, old chap. Sit up."

Monkhouse Lee had raised himself on his hands and looked wildly about him.

"What's up?" he asked. "I've been in the water. Ah, yes; I remember."

A look of fear came into his eyes, and he sank his face into his hands.

"How did you fall in?"

"I didn't fall in."

"How, then?"

"I was thrown in. I was standing by the bank, and something from behind picked me up like a feather and hurled me in. I heard nothing, and I saw nothing. But I know what it was, for all that."

"And so do I," whispered Smith.

Lee looked up with a quick glance of surprise. "You've learned, then!" he said. "You remember the advice I gave you?"

"Yes, and I begin to think that I shall take it."

"I don't know what the deuce you fellows are talking about," said Hastie, "but I think, if I were you, Harrington, I should get Lee to bed at once. It will be time enough to discuss the why and the wherefore when he is a little stronger. I think, Smith, you and I can leave him alone now. I am walking back to college; if you are coming in that direction, we can have a chat."

But it was little chat that they had upon their homeward path. Smith's mind was too full of the incidents of the evening, the absence of the mummy from his neighbour's rooms, the step that passed him on the stair, the reappearance—the extraordinary, inexplicable reappearance of the grisly thing—and then this attack upon Lee, corresponding so closely to the previous outrage upon another man against whom Bellingham bore a grudge. All this settled in his thoughts, together with the many little incidents which had previously turned him against his neighbour, and the singular circumstances under which he was first called in to him. What had been a dim suspicion, a vague, fantastic conjecture, had suddenly taken form, and stood out in his mind as a grim fact, a thing not to be denied. And yet, how monstrous it was! how unheard of! how entirely beyond all bounds of human experience. An impartial judge, or even the friend who walked by his side, would simply tell him that his eyes had deceived him, that the mummy had been there all the time, that young Lee had tumbled into the river as any other man tumbles into a river, and that a blue pill was the best thing for a disordered liver. He felt that he would have said as much if the positions had been reversed. And yet he could swear that Bellingham was a murderer at heart, and that he wielded a weapon such as no man had ever used in all the grim history of crime.

Hastie had branched off to his rooms with a few crisp and emphatic comments upon his friend's unsociability, and Abercrombie Smith crossed the quadrangle to his corner turret with a strong feeling of repulsion for his chambers and their associations. He would take Lee's advice, and move his quarters as soon as possible, for how could a man study when his ear was ever straining for every murmur or footstep in the room below? He observed, as he crossed over the lawn, that the light was still shining in Bellingham's window, and as he passed up the staircase the door opened, and the man himself looked out at him. With his fat, evil face he was like some bloated spider fresh from the weaving of his poisonous web.

"Good-evening," said he. "Won't you come in?"

"No," cried Smith, fiercely.

"No? You are busy as ever? I wanted to ask you about Lee. I was sorry to hear that there was a rumour that something was amiss with him."

His features were grave, but there was the gleam of a hidden laugh in his eyes as he spoke. Smith saw it, and he could have knocked him down for it.

"You'll be sorrier still to hear that Monkhouse Lee is doing very well, and is out of all danger," he answered. "Your hellish tricks have not come off this time. Oh, you needn't try to brazen it out. I know all about it."

Bellingham took a step back from the angry student, and half-closed the door as if to protect himself.

"You are mad," he said. "What do you mean? Do you assert that I had anything to do with Lee's accident?"

"Yes," thundered Smith. "You and that bag of bones behind you; you worked it between you. I tell you what it is, Master B., they have given up burning folk like you, but we still keep a hangman, and, by George! if any man in this college meets his death while you are here, I'll have you up, and if you don't swing for it, it won't be my fault. You'll find that your filthy Egyptian tricks won't answer in England."

"You're a raving lunatic," said Bellingham.

"All right. You just remember what I say, for you'll find that I'll be better than my word."

The door slammed, and Smith went fuming up to his chamber, where he locked the door upon the inside, and spent half the night in smoking his old briar and brooding over the strange events of the evening.

Next morning Abercrombie Smith heard nothing of his neighbour, but Harrington called upon him in the afternoon to say that Lee was almost himself again. All day Smith stuck fast to his work, but in the evening he determined to pay the visit to his friend Dr. Peterson upon which he had started upon the night before. A good walk and a friendly chat would be welcome to his jangled nerves.

Bellingham's door was shut as he passed, but glancing back when he was some distance from the turret, he saw his neighbour's head at the window outlined against the lamp-light, his face pressed apparently against the glass as he gazed out into the darkness. It was a blessing to be away from all contact with him, but if for a few hours, and Smith stepped out briskly, and breathed the soft spring air into his lungs. The half-moon lay in the west between two Gothic pinnacles and threw upon the silvered street a dark tracery from the stone-work above. There was a brisk breeze, and light, fleecy clouds drifted swiftly across the sky. Old's was on the very border of the town and in five minutes Smith found himself beyond the houses and between the hedges of a May-scented Oxfordshire lane.

It was a lonely and little frequented road which led to his friend's house. Early as it was, Smith did not meet a single soul upon his way. He walked briskly along until he came to the avenue gate, which opened into the long gravel drive leading up to Farlingford. In front of him he could see the cosy red light of the windows glimmering through the foliage. He stood with his hand upon the iron latch of the swinging gate, and he glanced back at the road along which he had come. Something was coming swiftly down it.

It moved in the shadow of the hedge, silently and furtively, a dark, crouching figure, dimly visible against the black background. Even as he gazed back at it, it had lessened its distance by twenty paces and was fast closing upon him. Out of the darkness he had a glimpse of a scraggy neck, and of two eyes that will ever haunt him in his dreams. He turned, and with a cry of terror he ran for his life up the avenue. There were the red lights, the signals of safety, almost within a stone's throw of him. He was a famous runner, but never had he run as he ran that night.

The heavy gate had swung into place behind him, but he heard it dash open again before his pursuer. As he rushed madly and wildly through the night, he could hear a swift, dry patter behind him, and could see, as he threw back a glance, that this horror was bounding like a tiger at his heels, with blazing eyes and one stringy arm outthrown. Thank God, the door was ajar. He could see the thin bar of light which shot from the lamp in the hall. Nearer yet sounded the clatter from behind. He heard a hoarse gurgling at his very shoulder. With a shriek he flung himself against the door, slammed and bolted it behind him, and sank half-fainting on to the hall chair.

"My goodness, Smith, what's the matter?" asked Peterson, appearing at the door of his study.

"Give me some brandy!"

Peterson disappeared and came rushing out again with a glass and a decanter.

"You need it," he said, as his visitor drank off what he poured out for him. "Why, man, you are as white as a cheese."

Smith laid down his glass, rose up, and took a deep breath.

"I am my own man again now," said he. "I was never so unmanned before. But, with your leave, Peterson, I will sleep here tonight, for I don't think I could face that road again except by daylight. It's weak, I know, but I can't help it."

Peterson looked at his visitor with a very questioning eye.

"Of course, you shall sleep here if you wish. I'll tell Mrs. Burney to make up the spare bed. Where are you off to now?"

"Come up with me to the window that overlooks the door. I want you to see what I have seen."

They went up to the window of the upper hall whence they could look down upon the approach to the house. The drive and the fields on either side lay quiet and still, bathed in the peaceful moonlight.

"Well, really, Smith," remarked Peterson, "it is well that I know you to be an abstemious man. What in the world can have frightened you?"

"I'll tell you presently. But where can it have gone? Ah, now look, look! See the curve of the road just beyond your gate."

"Yes, I see; you needn't pinch my arm off. I saw someone pass. I should say a man, rather thin, apparently, and tall, very tall. But what of him? And what of yourself? You are still shaking like an aspen leaf."

"I have been within hand-grip of the devil, that's all. But come down to your study, and I shall tell you the whole story."

He did so. Under the cheery lamplight, with a glass of wine on the table beside him, and the portly form and florid face of his friend in front, he narrated, in their order, all the events, great and small, which had formed so singular a chain, from the night on which he had found Bellingham fainting in front of the mummy case until his horrid experience of an hour ago.

"There now," he said as he concluded, "that's the whole black business. It is monstrous and incredible, but it is true."

Dr. Plumptree Peterson sat for some time in silence with a very puzzled expression upon his face.

"I never heard of such a thing in my life, never!" he said at last. "You have told me the facts. Now tell me your inferences."

"You can draw your own."

"But I should like to hear yours. You have thought over the matter, and I have not."

"Well, it must be a little vague in detail, but the main points seem to me to be clear enough. This fellow Bellingham, in his Eastern studies, has got hold of some infernal secret by which a mummy—or possibly only this particular mummy—can be temporarily brought to life. He was trying this disgusting business on the night when he fainted. No doubt the sight of the creature moving had shaken his nerve, even though he had expected it. You remember that almost the first words he said were to call out upon himself as a fool. Well, he got more hardened afterwards and carried the matter through without fainting. The vitality which he could put into it was evidently only a passing thing, for I have seen it continually in its case as dead as this table. He has some elaborate process, I fancy, by which he brings the thing to pass. Having done it, he naturally bethought him that he might use the creature as an agent. It has intelligence and it has strength. For some purpose he took Lee into his confidence; but Lee, like a decent Christian, would have nothing to do with such a business. Then they had a row, and Lee vowed that he would tell his sister of Bellingham's true character. Bellingham's game was to prevent him, and he nearly managed it, by setting this creature of his on his track. He had already tried its powers upon another man—Norton—towards whom he had a grudge. It is the merest chance that he has not two murders upon his soul. Then, when I taxed him with the matter, he had the strongest reasons for wishing to get me out of the way before I could convey my knowledge to anyone else. He got his chance when I went out, for he knew my habits, and where I was bound for. I have had a narrow shave, Peterson, and it is mere luck you didn't find me on your doorstep in the morning. I'm not a nervous man as a rule, and I never thought to have the fear of death put upon me as it was tonight."

"My dear boy, you take the matter too seriously," said his companion. "Your nerves are out of order with your work, and you make too much of it. How could such a thing as this stride about the streets of Oxford, even at night, without being seen?"

"It has been seen. There is quite a scare in the town about an escaped ape, as they imagine the creature to be. It is the talk of the place."

"Well, it's a striking chain of events. And yet, my dear fellow, you must allow that each incident in itself is capable of a more natural explanation."

"What! even my adventure of tonight?"

"Certainly. You come out with your nerves all unstrung, and your head full of this theory of yours. Some gaunt, half-famished tramp steals after you, and seeing you run, is emboldened to pursue you. Your fears and imagination do the rest."

"It won't do, Peterson; it won't do."

"And again, in the instance of your finding the mummy case empty, and then a few moments later with an occupant, you know that it was lamplight, that the lamp was half turned down, and that you had no special reason to look hard at the case. It is quite possible that you may have overlooked the creature in the first instance."

"No, no; it is out of the question."

"And then Lee may have fallen into the river, and Norton been garrotted. It is certainly a formidable indictment that you have against Bellingham; but if you were to place it before a police magistrate, he would simply laugh in your face."

"I know he would. That is why I mean to take the matter into my own hands."

"Eh?"

"Yes; I feel that a public duty rests upon me, and, besides, I must do it for my own safety, unless I choose to allow myself to be hunted by this beast out of the college, and that would be a little too feeble. I have quite made up my mind what I shall do. And first of all, may I use your paper and pens for an hour?"

"Most certainly. You will find all that you want upon that side table."

Abercrombie Smith sat down before a sheet of foolscap, and for an hour, and then for a second hour his pen travelled swiftly over it. Page after page was finished and tossed aside while his friend leaned back in his arm-chair, looking across at him with patient curiosity. At last, with an exclamation of satisfaction, Smith sprang to his feet, gathered his papers up into order, and laid the last one upon Peterson's desk.

"Kindly sign this as a witness," he said.

"A witness? Of what?"

"Of my signature, and of the date. The date is the most important. Why, Peterson, my life might hang upon it."

"My dear Smith, you are talking wildly. Let me beg you to go to bed."

"On the contrary, I never spoke so deliberately in my life. And I will promise to go to bed the moment you have signed it."

"But what is it?"

"It is a statement of all that I have been telling you tonight. I wish you to witness it."

"Certainly," said Peterson, signing his name under that of his companion. "There you are! But what is the idea?"

"You will kindly retain it and produce it in case I am arrested."

"Arrested? For what?"

"For murder. It is quite on the cards. I wish to be ready for every event. There is only one course open to me, and I am determined to take it."

"For Heaven's sake, don't do anything rash!"

"Believe me, it would be far more rash to adopt any other course. I hope that we won't need to bother you, but it will ease my mind to know that you have this statement of my motives. And now I am ready to take your advice and to go to roost, for I want to be at my best in the morning."

Abercrombie Smith was not an entirely pleasant man to have as an enemy. Slow and easy tempered, he was formidable when driven to action. He brought to every purpose in life the same deliberate resoluteness which had distinguished him as a scientific student. He had laid his studies aside for a day, but he intended that the day should not be wasted. Not a word did he say to his host as to his plans, but by nine o'clock he was well on his way to Oxford.

In the High Street he stopped at Clifford's, the gun-makers and bought a heavy revolver, with a box of central-fire cartridges. Six of them he slipped into the chambers, and half-cocking the weapon, placed it in the pocket of his coat. He then made his way to Hastie's rooms, where the big oarsman was lounging over his breakfast, with the Sporting Times propped up against the coffeepot.

"Hullo! What's up?" he asked. "Have some coffee?"

"No, thank you. I want you to come with me, Hastie, and do what I ask you."

"Certainly, my boy."

"And bring a heavy stick with you."

"Hullo!" Hastie stared. "Here's a hunting-crop that would fell an ox."

"One other thing. You have a box of amputating knives. Give me the longest of them."

"There you are. You seem to be fairly on the war trail. Anything else?"

"No; that will do." Smith placed the knife inside his coat and led the way to the quadrangle. "We are neither of us chickens, Hastie," said he. "I think I can do this job alone, but I take you as a precaution. I am going to have a little talk with Bellingham. If I have only him to deal with, I won't, of course, need you. If I shout, however, up you come, and lam out with your whip as hard as you can lick. Do you understand?"

"All right. I'll come if I hear you bellow."

"Stay here, then. It may be a little time, but don't budge until I come down."

"I'm a fixture."

Smith ascended the stairs, opened Bellingham's door and stepped in. Bellingham was seated behind his table, writing. Beside him, among his litter of strange possessions, towered the mummy case, with its sale number 249 still stuck upon its front, and its hideous occupant stiff and stark within it. Smith looked very deliberately round him, closed the door, locked it, took the key from the inside, and then stepping across to the fireplace, struck a match and set the fire alight. Bellingham sat staring, with amazement and rage upon his bloated face.

"Well, really now, you make yourself at home," he gasped.

Smith sat himself deliberately down, placing his watch upon the table, drew out his pistol, cocked it, and laid it in his lap. Then he took the long amputating knife from his bosom and threw it down in front of Bellingham.

"Now, then," said he, "just get to work and cut up that mummy."

"Oh, is that it?" said Bellingham with a sneer.

"Yes, that is it. They tell me that the law can't touch you. But I have a law that will set matters straight. If in five minutes you have not set to work, I swear by the God who made me that I will put a bullet through your brain!"

"You would murder me?"

Bellingham had half risen, and his face was the colour of putty.

"Yes."

"And for what?"

"To stop your mischief. One minute has gone."

"But what have I done?"

"I know and you know."

"This is mere bullying."

"Two minutes are gone."

"But you must give reasons. You are a madman—a dangerous madman. Why should I destroy my own property? It is a valuable mummy."

"You must cut it up, and you must burn it."

"I will do no such thing."

"Four minutes are gone."

Smith took up the pistol and he looked towards Bellingham with an inexorable face. As the second-hand stole round, he raised his hand, and the finger twitched upon the trigger.

"There! there! I'll do it!" screamed Bellingham.

In frantic haste he caught up the knife and hacked at the figure of the mummy, ever glancing round to see the eye and the weapon of his terrible visitor bent upon him. The creature crackled and snapped under every stab of the keen blade. A thick yellow dust rose up from it. Spices and dried essences rained down upon the floor. Suddenly, with a rending crack, its backbone snapped asunder, and it fell, a brown heap of sprawling limbs, upon the floor.

"Now into the fire!" said Smith.

The flames leaped and roared as the dried and tinder like debris was piled upon it. The little room was like the stoke-hole of a steamer and the sweat ran down the faces of the two men; but still the one stooped and worked, while the other sat watching him with a set face. A thick, fat smoke oozed out from the fire, and a heavy smell of burned rosin and singed hair filled the air. In a quarter of an hour a few charred and brittle sticks were all that was left of Lot No. 249.

"Perhaps that will satisfy you," snarled Bellingham, with hate and fear in his little grey eyes as he glanced back at his tormenter.

"No; I must make a clean sweep of all your materials. We must have no more devil's tricks. In with all these leaves! They may have something to do with it."

"And what now?" asked Bellingham, when the leaves also had been added to the blaze.

"Now the roll of papyrus which you had on the table that night. It is in that drawer, I think."

"No, no," shouted Bellingham. "Don't burn that! Why, man, you don't know what you do. It is unique; it contains wisdom which is nowhere else to be found."

"Out with it!"

"But look here, Smith, you can't really mean it. I'll share the knowledge with you. I'll teach you all that is in it. Or stay, let me only copy it before you burn it!"

Smith stepped forward and turned the key in the drawer. Taking out the yellow, curled roll of paper, he threw it into the fire and pressed it down with his heel. Bellingham screamed and grabbed at it; but Smith pushed him back and stood over it until it was reduced to a formless grey ash.

"Now, Master B.," said he, "I think I have pretty well drawn your teeth. You'll hear from me again, if you return to your old tricks. And now good-morning, for I must go back to my studies."

And such is the narrative of Abercrombie Smith as to the singular events which occurred in Old College, Oxford, in the spring of '84. As Bellingham left the university immediately afterwards, and was last heard of in the Soudan, there is no one who can contradict his statement. But the wisdom of men is small, and the ways of nature are strange, and who shall put a bound to the dark things which may be found by those who seek for them?

THE HORROR OF THE HEIGHTS

The idea that the extraordinary narrative which has been called the Joyce-Armstrong Fragment is an elaborate practical joke evolved by some unknown person, cursed by a perverted and sinister sense of humour, has now been abandoned by all who have examined the matter. The most macabre and imaginative of plotters would hesitate before linking his morbid fancies with the unquestioned and tragic facts which reinforce the statement. Though the assertions contained in it are amazing and even monstrous, it is none the less forcing itself upon the general intelligence that they are true, and that we must readjust our ideas to the new situation. This world of ours appears to be separated by a slight and precarious margin of safety from a most singular and unexpected danger. I will endeavour in this narrative, which reproduces the original document in its necessarily somewhat fragmentary form, to lay before the reader the whole of the facts up to date, prefacing my statement by saying that, if there be any who doubt the narrative of Joyce-Armstrong, there can be no question at all as to the facts concerning Lieutenant Myrtle, R. N., and Mr. Hay Connor, who undoubtedly met their end in the manner described.

The Joyce-Armstrong Fragment was found in the field, which is called Lower Haycock, lying one mile to the westward of the village of Withyham, upon the Kent and Sussex border. It was on the 15th September last that an agricultural labourer, James Flynn, in the employment of Mathew Dodd, farmer, of the Chauntry Farm, Withyham, perceived a briar pipe lying near the footpath which skirts the hedge in Lower Haycock. A few paces farther on he picked up a pair of broken binocular glasses. Finally, among some nettles in the ditch, he caught sight of a flat, canvas-backed book, which proved to be a note-book with detachable leaves, some of which had come loose and were fluttering along the base of the hedge. These he collected, but some, including the first, were never recovered, and leave a deplorable hiatus in this all-important statement. The note-book was taken by the labourer to his master, who in turn showed it to Dr. J. H. Atherton, of Hartfield. This gentleman at once recognized the need for an expert examination, and the manuscript was forwarded to the Aero Club in London, where it now lies.

The first two pages of the manuscript are missing. There is also one torn away at the end of the narrative, though none of these affect the general coherence of the story. It is conjectured that the missing opening is concerned with the record of Mr. Joyce-Armstrong's qualifications as an aeronaut, which can be gathered from other sources and are admitted to be unsurpassed among the air-pilots of England. For many years he has been looked upon as among the most daring and the most intellectual of flying men, a combination which has enabled him to both invent and test several new devices, including the common gyroscopic attachment which is known by his name. The main body of the manuscript is written neatly in ink, but the last few lines are in pencil and are so ragged as to be hardly legible—exactly, in fact, as they might be expected to appear if they were scribbled off hurriedly from the seat of a moving aeroplane. There are, it may be added, several stains, both on the last page and on the outside cover which have been pronounced by the Home Office experts to be blood—probably human and certainly mammalian. The fact that something closely resembling the organism of malaria was discovered in this blood, and that Joyce-Armstrong is known to have suffered from intermittent fever, is a remarkable example of the new weapons which modern science has placed in the hands of our detectives.

And now a word as to the personality of the author of this epoch-making statement. Joyce-Armstrong, according to the few friends who really knew something of the man, was a poet and a dreamer, as well as a mechanic and an inventor. He was a man of considerable wealth, much of which he had spent in the pursuit of his aeronautical hobby. He had four private aeroplanes in his hangars near Devizes and is said to have made no fewer than one hundred and seventy ascents in the course of last year. He was a retiring man with dark moods, in which he would avoid the society of his fellows. Captain Dangerfield, who knew him better than anyone, says that there were times when his eccentricity threatened to develop into something more serious. His habit of carrying a shot-gun with him in his aeroplane was one manifestation of it.

Another was the morbid effect which the fall of Lieutenant Myrtle had upon his mind. Myrtle, who was attempting the height record, fell from an altitude of something over thirty thousand feet. Horrible to narrate, his head was entirely obliterated, though his body and limbs preserved their configuration. At every gathering of airmen, Joyce-Armstrong, according to Dangerfield, would ask, with an enigmatic smile: "And where, pray, is Myrtle's head?"

On another occasion after dinner, at the mess of the Flying School on Salisbury Plain, he started a debate as to what will be the most permanent danger which airmen will have to encounter. Having listened to successive opinions as to air-pockets, faulty construction, and over-banking, he ended by shrugging his shoulders and refusing to put forward his own views, though he gave the impression that they differed from any advanced by his companions.

It is worth remarking that after his own complete disappearance it was found that his private affairs were arranged with a precision which may show that he had a strong premonition of disaster. With these essential explanations I will now give the narrative exactly as it stands, beginning at page three of the blood-soaked note-book:

"Nevertheless, when I dined at Rheims with Coselli and Gustav Raymond I found that neither of them was aware of any particular danger in the higher layers of the atmosphere. I did not actually say what was in my thoughts, but I got so near to it that if they had any corresponding idea they could not have failed to express it. But then they are two empty, vainglorious fellows with no thought beyond seeing their silly names in the newspaper. It is interesting to note that neither of them had ever been much beyond the twenty-thousand-foot level. Of course, men have been higher than this both in balloons and in the ascent of mountains. It must be well above that point that the aeroplane enters the danger zone—always presuming that my premonitions are correct.

"Aeroplaning has been with us now for more than twenty years, and one might well ask: Why should this peril be only revealing itself in our day? The answer is obvious. In the old days of weak engines, when a hundred horse-power Gnome or Green was considered ample for every need, the flights were very restricted. Now that three hundred horse-power is the rule rather than the exception, visits to the upper layers have become easier and more common. Some of us can remember how, in our youth, Garros made a world-wide reputation by attaining nineteen thousand feet, and it was considered a remarkable achievement to fly over the Alps. Our standard now has been immeasurably raised, and there are twenty high flights for one in former years. Many of them have been undertaken with impunity. The thirty-thousand-foot level has been reached time after time with no discomfort beyond cold and asthma. What does this prove? A visitor might descend upon this planet a thousand times and never see a tiger. Yet tigers exist, and if he chanced to come down into a jungle he might be devoured. There are jungles of the upper air, and there are worse things than tigers which inhabit them. I believe in time they will map these jungles accurately out. Even at the present moment I could name two of them. One of them lies over the Pau-Biarritz district of France. Another is just over my head as I write here in my house in Wiltshire. I rather think there is a third in the Homburg-Wiesbaden district.

"It was the disappearance of the airmen that first set me thinking. Of course, everyone said that they had fallen into the sea, but that did not satisfy me at all. First, there was Verrier in France; his machine was found near Bayonne, but they never got his body. There was the case of Baxter also, who vanished, though his engine and some of the iron fixings were found in a wood in Leicestershire. In that case, Dr. Middleton, of Amesbury, who was watching the flight with a telescope, declares that just before the clouds obscured the view he saw the machine, which was at an enormous height, suddenly rise perpendicularly upwards in a succession of jerks in a manner that he would have thought to be impossible. That was the last seen of Baxter. There was a correspondence in the papers, but it never led to anything. There were several other similar cases, and then there was the death of Hay Connor. What a cackle there was about an unsolved mystery of the air, and what columns in the halfpenny papers, and yet how little was ever done to get to the bottom of the business! He came down in a tremendous vol-plane from an unknown height. He never got off his machine and died in his pilot's seat. Died of what? 'Heart disease,' said the doctors. Rubbish! Hay Connor's heart was as sound as mine is. What did Venables say? Venables was the only man who was at his side when he died. He said that he was shivering and looked like a man who had been badly scared. 'Died of fright,' said Venables, but could not imagine what he was frightened about. Only said one word to Venables, which sounded like 'Monstrous.' They could make nothing of that at the inquest. But I could make something of it. Monsters! That was the last word of poor Harry Hay Connor. And he did die of fright, just as Venables thought.

"And then there was Myrtle's head. Do you really believe—does anybody really believe—that a man's head could be driven clean into his body by the force of a fall? Well, perhaps it may be possible, but I, for one, have never believed that it was so with Myrtle. And the grease upon his clothes—'all slimy with grease,' said somebody at the inquest. Queer that nobody got thinking after that! I did—but then, I had been thinking for a good long time. I've made three ascents—how Dangerfield used to chaff me about my shot-gun—but I've never been high enough. Now, with this new, light Paul Veroner machine and its one hundred and seventy-five Robur, I should easily touch the thirty thousand tomorrow. I'll have a shot at the record. Maybe I shall have a shot at something else as well. Of course, it's dangerous. If a fellow wants to avoid danger he had best keep out of flying altogether and subside finally into flannel slippers and a dressing-gown. But I'll visit the air-jungle tomorrow—and if there's anything there I shall know it. If I return, I'll find myself a bit of a celebrity. If I don't this note-book may explain what I am trying to do, and how I lost my life in doing it. But no drivel about accidents or mysteries, if you please.

"I chose my Paul Veroner monoplane for the job. There's nothing like a monoplane when real work is to be done. Beaumont found that out in very early days. For one thing it doesn't mind damp, and the weather looks as if we should be in the clouds all the time. It's a bonny little model and answers my hand like a tender-mouthed horse. The engine is a ten-cylinder rotary Robur working up to one hundred and seventy-five. It has all the modern improvements—enclosed fuselage, high-curved landing skids, brakes, gyroscopic steadier's and three speeds, worked by an alteration of the angle of the planes upon the Venetian-blind principle. I took a shot-gun with me and a dozen cartridges filled with buck-shot. You should have seen the face of Perkins, my old mechanic, when I directed him to put them in. I was dressed like an Arctic explorer, with two jerseys under my overalls, thick socks inside my padded boots, a storm-cap with flaps, and my talc goggles. It was stifling outside the hangars, but I was going for the summit of the Himalayas and had to dress for the part. Perkins knew there was something on and implored me to take him with me. Perhaps I should if I were using the biplane, but a monoplane is a one-man show—if you want to get the last foot of life out of it. Of course, I took an oxygen bag; the man who goes for the altitude record without one will either be frozen or smothered—or both.

"I had a good look at the planes, the rudder-bar, and the elevating lever before I got in. Everything was in order so far as I could see. Then I switched on my engine and found that she was running sweetly. When they let her go she rose almost at once upon the lowest speed. I circled my home field once or twice just to warm her up, and then with a wave to Perkins and the others, I flattened out my planes and put her on her highest. She skimmed like a swallow downwind for eight or ten miles until I turned her nose up a little and she began to climb in a great spiral for the cloud-bank above me. It's all-important to rise slowly and adapt yourself to the pressure as you go.

"It was a close, warm day for an English September, and there was the hush and heaviness of impending rain. Now and then there came sudden puffs of wind from the south-west—one of them so gusty and unexpected that it caught me napping and turned me half-round for an instant. I remember the time when gusts and whirls and air-pockets used to be things of danger—before we learned to put an overmastering power into our engines. Just as I reached the cloud-banks, with the altimeter marking three thousand, down came the rain. My word, how it poured! It drummed upon my wings and lashed against my face, blurring my glasses so that I could hardly see. I got down on to a low speed, for it was painful to travel against it. As I got higher it became hail, and I had to turn tail to it. One of my cylinders was out of action—a dirty plug, I should imagine, but still I was rising steadily with plenty of power. After a bit the trouble passed, whatever it was, and I heard the full, deep-throated purr—the ten singing as one. That's where the beauty of our modern silencers comes in. We can at last control our engines by ear. How they squeal and squeak and sob when they are in trouble! All those cries for help were wasted in the old days, when every sound was swallowed up by the monstrous racket of the machine. If only the early aviators could come back to see the beauty and perfection of the mechanism which have been bought at the cost of their lives!

"About nine-thirty I was nearing the clouds. Down below me, all blurred and shadowed with rain, lay the vast expanse of Salisbury Plain. Half a dozen flying machines were doing hackwork at the thousand-foot level, looking like little black swallows against the green background. I dare say they were wondering what I was doing up in cloud-land. Suddenly a grey curtain drew across beneath me and the wet folds of vapours were swirling round my face. It was clammily cold and miserable. But I was above the hail-storm, and that was something gained. The cloud was as dark and thick as a London fog. In my anxiety to get clear, I cocked her nose up until the automatic alarm-bell rang, and I actually began to slide backwards. My sopped and dripping wings had made me heavier than I thought, but presently I was in lighter cloud, and soon had cleared the first layer. There was a second—opal-coloured and fleecy—at a great height above my head, a white, unbroken ceiling above, and a dark, unbroken floor below, with the monoplane labouring upwards upon a vast spiral between them. It is deadly lonely in these cloud-spaces. Once a great flight of some small water-birds went past me, flying very fast to the westwards. The quick whir of their wings and their musical cry were cheery to my ear. I fancy that they were teal, but I am a wretched zoologist. Now that we humans have become birds we must really learn to know our brethren by sight.

"The wind down beneath me whirled and swayed the broad cloud-plain. Once a great eddy formed in it, a whirlpool of vapour and through it, as down a funnel, I caught sight of the distant world. A large white biplane was passing at a vast depth beneath me. I fancy it was the morning mail service betwixt Bristol and London. Then the drift swirled inwards again and the great solitude was unbroken.

"Just after ten I touched the lower edge of the upper cloud-stratum. It consisted of fine diaphanous vapour drifting swiftly from the westwards. The wind had been steadily rising all this time and it was now blowing a sharp breeze—twenty-eight an hour by my gauge. Already it was very cold, though my altimeter only marked nine thousand. The engines were working beautifully, and we went droning steadily upwards. The cloud-bank was thicker than I had expected, but at last it thinned out into a golden mist before me, and then in an instant I had shot out from it, and there was an unclouded sky and a brilliant sun above my head—all blue and gold above, all shining silver below, one vast, glimmering plain as far as my eyes could reach. It was a quarter past ten o'clock, and the barograph needle pointed to twelve thousand eight hundred. Up I went and up, my ears concentrated upon the deep purring of my motor, my eyes busy always with the watch, the revolution indicator, the petrol lever, and the oil pump. No wonder aviators are said to be a fearless race. With so many things to think of there is no time to trouble about oneself. About this time, I noted how unreliable is the compass when above a certain height from earth. At fifteen thousand feet mine was pointing east and a point south. The sun and the wind gave me my true bearings.

"I had hoped to reach an eternal stillness in these high altitudes, but with every thousand feet of ascent the gale grew stronger. My machine groaned and trembled in every joint and rivet as she faced it and swept away like a sheet of paper when I banked her on the turn, skimming downwind at a greater pace, perhaps, than ever mortal man has moved. Yet I had always to turn again and tack up in the wind's eye, for it was not merely a height record that I was after. By all my calculations it was above little Wiltshire that my air-jungle lay, and all my labour might be lost if I struck the outer layers at some farther point.

"When I reached the nineteen-thousand-foot level, which was about midday, the wind was so severe that I looked with some anxiety to the stays of my wings, expecting momentarily to see them snap or slacken. I even cast loose the parachute behind me and fastened its hook into the ring of my leathern belt, so as to be ready for the worst. Now was the time when a bit of scamped work by the mechanic is paid for by the life of the aeronaut. But she held together bravely. Every cord and strut was humming and vibrating like so many harp-strings, but it was glorious to see how, for all the beating and the buffeting, she was still the conqueror of Nature and the mistress of the sky. There is surely something divine in man himself that he should rise so superior to the limitations which Creation seemed to impose—rise, too, by such unselfish, heroic devotion as this air-conquest has shown. Talk of human degeneration! When has such a story as this been written in the annals of our race?

"These were the thoughts in my head as I climbed that monstrous, inclined plane with the wind sometimes beating in my face and sometimes whistling behind my ears, while the cloud-land beneath me fell away to such a distance that the folds and hummocks of silver had all smoothed out into one flat, shining plain. But suddenly I had a horrible and unprecedented experience. I have known before what it is to be in what our neighbours have called a tourbillon, but never on such a scale as this. That huge, sweeping river of wind of which I have spoken had, as it appears, whirlpools within it which were as monstrous as itself. Without a moment's warning I was dragged suddenly into the heart of one. I spun round for a minute or two with such velocity that I almost lost my senses, and then fell suddenly, left wing foremost, down the vacuum funnel in the centre. I dropped like a stone and lost nearly a thousand feet. It was only my belt that kept me in my seat, and the shock and breathlessness left me hanging half-insensible over the side of the fuselage. But I am always capable of a supreme effort—it is my one great merit as an aviator. I was conscious that the descent was slower. The whirlpool was a cone rather than a funnel, and I had come to the apex. With a terrific wrench, throwing my weight all to one side, I levelled my planes and brought her head away from the wind. In an instant I had shot out of the eddies and was skimming down the sky. Then, shaken but victorious, I turned her nose up and began once more my steady grind on the upward spiral. I took a large sweep to avoid the danger-spot of the whirlpool, and soon I was safely above it. Just after one o'clock I was twenty-one thousand feet above the sea-level. To my great joy I had topped the gale, and with every hundred feet of ascent the air grew stiller. On the other hand, it was very cold, and I was conscious of that peculiar nausea which goes with rarefaction of the air. For the first time I unscrewed the mouth of my oxygen bag and took an occasional whiff of the glorious gas. I could feel it running like a cordial through my veins, and I was exhilarated almost to the point of drunkenness. I shouted and sang as I soared upwards into the cold, still outer world.

"It is very clear to me that the insensibility which came upon Glaisher and in a lesser degree upon Coxwell, when, in 1862, they ascended in a balloon to the height of thirty thousand feet, was due to the extreme speed with which a perpendicular ascent is made. Doing it at an easy gradient and accustoming oneself to the lessened barometric pressure by slow degrees, there are no such dreadful symptoms. At the same great height, I found that even without my oxygen inhaler I could breathe without undue distress. It was bitterly cold, however, and my thermometer was at zero, Fahrenheit. At one-thirty I was nearly seven miles above the surface of the earth, and still ascending steadily. I found, however, that the rarefied air was giving markedly less support to my planes, and that my angle of ascent had to be considerably lowered in consequence. It was already clear that even with my light weight and strong engine-power there was a point in front of me where I should be held. To make matters worse, one of my sparking-plugs was in trouble again and there was intermittent misfiring in the engine. My heart was heavy with the fear of failure.

"It was about that time that I had a most extraordinary experience. Something whizzed past me in a trail of smoke and exploded with a loud, hissing sound, sending forth a cloud of steam. For the instant I could not imagine what had happened. Then I remembered that the earth is forever being bombarded by meteor stones and would be hardly inhabitable were they not in nearly every case turned to vapour in the outer layers of the atmosphere. Here is a new danger for the high-altitude man, for two others passed me when I was nearing the forty-thousand-foot mark. I cannot doubt that at the edge of the earth's envelope the risk would be a very real one.

"My barograph needle marked forty-one thousand three hundred when I became aware that I could go no farther. Physically, the strain was not as yet greater than I could bear but my machine had reached its limit. The attenuated air gave no firm support to the wings, and the least tilt developed into side-slip, while she seemed sluggish on her controls. Possibly, had the engine been at its best, another thousand feet might have been within our capacity, but it was still misfiring, and two out of the ten cylinders appeared to be out of action. If I had not already reached the zone for which I was searching then I should never see it upon this journey. But was it not possible that I had attained it? Soaring in circles like a monstrous hawk upon the forty-thousand-foot level I let the monoplane guide herself, and with my Mannheim glass I made a careful observation of my surroundings. The heavens were perfectly clear; there was no indication of those dangers which I had imagined.

"I have said that I was soaring in circles. It struck me suddenly that I would do well to take a wider sweep and open up a new air tract. If the hunter entered an earth-jungle he would drive through it if he wished to find his game. My reasoning had led me to believe that the air-jungle which I had imagined lay somewhere over Wiltshire. This should be to the south and west of me. I took my bearings from the sun, for the compass was hopeless and no trace of earth was to be seen—nothing but the distant, silver cloud-plain. However, I got my direction as best I might and kept her head straight to the mark. I reckoned that my petrol supply would not last for more than another hour or so, but I could afford to use it to the last drop, since a single magnificent vol-plane could at any time take me to the earth.

"Suddenly I was aware of something new. The air in front of me had lost its crystal clearness. It was full of long, ragged wisps of something which I can only compare to very fine cigarette smoke. It hung about in wreaths and coils, turning and twisting slowly in the sunlight. As the monoplane shot through it, I was aware of a faint taste of oil upon my lips, and there was a greasy scum upon the woodwork of the machine. Some infinitely fine organic matter appeared to be suspended in the atmosphere. There was no life there. It was inchoate and diffuse, extending for many square acres and then fringing off into the void. No, it was not life. But might it not be the remains of life? Above all, might it not be the food of life, of monstrous life, even as the humble grease of the ocean is the food for the mighty whale? The thought was in my mind when my eyes looked upwards, and I saw the most wonderful vision that ever man has seen. Can I hope to convey it to you even as I saw it myself last Thursday?

"Conceive a jelly-fish such as sails in our summer seas, bell-shaped and of enormous size—far larger, I should judge, than the dome of St. Paul's. It was of a light pink colour veined with a delicate green, but the whole huge fabric so tenuous that it was but a fairy outline against the dark blue sky. It pulsated with a delicate and regular rhythm. From it there depended two long, drooping, green tentacles, which swayed slowly backwards and forwards. This gorgeous vision passed gently with noiseless dignity over my head, as light and fragile as a soap-bubble, and drifted upon its stately way.

"I had half-turned my monoplane, that I might look after this beautiful creature, when, in a moment, I found myself amidst a perfect fleet of them, of all sizes, but none so large as the first. Some were quite small, but the majority about as big as an average balloon, and with much the same curvature at the top. There was in them a delicacy of texture and colouring which reminded me of the finest Venetian glass. Pale shades of pink and green were the prevailing tints, but all had a lovely iridescence where the sun shimmered through their dainty forms. Some hundreds of them drifted past me, a wonderful fairy squadron of strange unknown argosies of the sky—creatures whose forms and substance were so attuned to these pure heights that one could not conceive anything so delicate within actual sight or sound of earth.

"But soon my attention was drawn to a new phenomenon—the serpents of the outer air. These were long, thin, fantastic coils of vapour-like material, which turned and twisted with great speed, flying round and round at such a pace that the eyes could hardly follow them. Some of these ghost-like creatures were twenty or thirty feet long, but it was difficult to tell their girth, for their outline was so hazy that it seemed to fade away into the air around them. These air-snakes were of a very light grey or smoke colour, with some darker lines within, which gave the impression of a definite organism. One of them whisked past my very face, and I was conscious of a cold, clammy contact, but their composition was so unsubstantial that I could not connect them with any thought of physical danger, any more than the beautiful bell-like creatures which had preceded them. There was no more solidity in their frames than in the floating spume from a broken wave.

"But a more terrible experience was in store for me. Floating downwards from a great height there came a purplish patch of vapour, small as I saw it first, but rapidly enlarging as it approached me, until it appeared to be hundreds of square feet in size. Though fashioned of some transparent, jelly-like substance, it was none the less of much more definite outline and solid consistence than anything which I had seen before. There were more traces, too, of a physical organization, especially two vast, shadowy, circular plates upon either side, which may have been eyes, and a perfectly solid white projection between them which was as curved and cruel as the beak of a vulture.

"The whole aspect of this monster was formidable and threatening, and it kept changing its colour from a very light mauve to a dark, angry purple so thick that it cast a shadow as it drifted between my monoplane and the sun. On the upper curve of its huge body there were three great projections which I can only describe as enormous bubbles, and I was convinced as I looked at them that they were charged with some extremely light gas which served to buoy up the misshapen and semi-solid mass in the rarefied air. The creature moved swiftly along, keeping pace easily with the monoplane, and for twenty miles or more it formed my horrible escort, hovering over me like a bird of prey which is waiting to pounce. Its method of progression— done so swiftly that it was not easy to follow—was to throw out a long, glutinous streamer in front of it, which in turn seemed to draw forward the rest of the writhing body. So elastic and gelatinous was it that never for two successive minutes was it the same shape, and yet each change made it more threatening and loathsome than the last.

"I knew that it meant mischief. Every purple flush of its hideous body told me so. The vague, goggling eyes which were turned always upon me were cold and merciless in their viscid hatred. I dipped the nose of my monoplane downwards to escape it. As I did so, as quick as a flash there shot out a long tentacle from this mass of floating blubber, and it fell as light and sinuous as a whip-lash across the front of my machine. There was a loud hiss as it lay for a moment across the hot engine, and it whisked itself into the air again, while the huge, flat body drew itself together as if in sudden pain. I dipped to a vol-pique, but again a tentacle fell over the monoplane and was shorn off by the propeller as easily as it might have cut through a smoke wreath. A long, gliding, sticky, serpent-like coil came from behind and caught me round the waist, dragging me out of the fuselage. I tore at it, my fingers sinking into the smooth, glue-like surface, and for an instant I disengaged myself, but only to be caught round the boot by another coil, which gave me a jerk that tilted me almost on to my back.

"As I fell over I blazed off both barrels of my gun, though, indeed, it was like attacking an elephant with a pea-shooter to imagine that any human weapon could cripple that mighty bulk. And yet I aimed better than I knew, for, with a loud report, one of the great blisters upon the creature's back exploded with the puncture of the buck-shot. It was very clear that my conjecture was right, and that these vast, clear bladders were distended with some lifting gas, for in an instant the huge, cloud-like body turned sideways, writhing desperately to find its balance, while the white beak snapped and gaped in horrible fury. But already I had shot away on the steepest glide that I dared to attempt, my engine still full on, the flying propeller and the force of gravity shooting me downwards like an aerolite. Far behind me I saw a dull, purplish smudge growing swiftly smaller and merging into the blue sky behind it. I was safe out of the deadly jungle of the outer air.

"Once out of danger I throttled my engine, for nothing tears a machine to pieces quicker than running on full power from a height. It was a glorious, spiral vol-plane from nearly eight miles of altitude—first, to the level of the silver cloud-bank, then to that of the storm-cloud beneath it, and finally, in beating rain, to the surface of the earth. I saw the Bristol Channel beneath me as I broke from the clouds, but, having still some petrol in my tank, I got twenty miles inland before I found myself stranded in a field half a mile from the village of Ashcombe. There I got three tins of petrol from a passing motor-car, and at ten minutes past six that evening I alighted gently in my own home meadow at Devizes, after such a journey as no mortal upon earth has ever yet taken and lived to tell the tale. I have seen the beauty, and I have seen the horror of the heights—and greater beauty or greater horror than that is not within the ken of man.

"And now it is my plan to go once again before I give my results to the world. My reason for this is that I must surely have something to show by way of proof before I lay such a tale before my fellow-men. It is true that others will soon follow and will confirm what I have said, and yet I should wish to carry conviction from the first. Those lovely iridescent bubbles of the air should not be hard to capture. They drift slowly upon their way, and the swift monoplane could intercept their leisurely course. It is likely enough that they would dissolve in the heavier layers of the atmosphere, and that some small heap of amorphous jelly might be all that I should bring to earth with me. And yet something there would surely be by which I could substantiate my story. Yes, I will go, even if I run a risk by doing so. These purple horrors would not seem to be numerous. It is probable that I shall not see one. If I do I shall dive at once. At the worst there is always the shot-gun and my knowledge of ..."

Here a page of the manuscript is unfortunately missing. On the next page is written, in large, straggling writing:

"Forty-three thousand feet. I shall never see earth again. They are beneath me, three of them. God help me; it is a dreadful death to die!"

Such in its entirety is the Joyce-Armstrong Statement. Of the man nothing has since been seen. Pieces of his shattered monoplane have been picked up in the preserves of Mr. Budd-Lushington upon the borders of Kent and Sussex, within a few miles of the spot where the note-book was discovered. If the unfortunate aviator's theory is correct that this air-jungle, as he called it, existed only over the south-west of England, then it would seem that he had fled from it at the full speed of his monoplane, but had been overtaken and devoured by these horrible creatures at some spot in the outer atmosphere above the place where the grim relics were found. The picture of that monoplane skimming down the sky, with the nameless terrors flying as swiftly beneath it and cutting it off always from the earth while they gradually closed in upon their victim, is one upon which a man who valued his sanity would prefer not to dwell. There are many, as I am aware, who still jeer at the facts which I have here set down, but even they must admit that Joyce-Armstrong has disappeared, and I would commend to them his own words: "This note-book may explain what

I am trying to do, and how I lost my life in doing it. But no drivel about accidents or mysteries, if you please."

THE DISAPPEARANCE OF LADY FRANCES CARFAX

"But why Turkish?" asked Mr. Sherlock Holmes, gazing fixedly at my boots. I was reclining in a cane-backed chair at the moment, and my protruded feet had attracted his ever-active attention.

"English," I answered in some surprise. "I got them at Latimer's, in Oxford Street."

Holmes smiled with an expression of weary patience.

"The bath!" he said, "the bath! Why the relaxing and expensive Turkish rather than the invigorating home-made article?"

"Because for the last few days I have been feeling rheumatic and old. A Turkish bath is what we call an alterative in medicine--a fresh starting-point, a cleanser of the system.

"By the way, Holmes," I added, "I have no doubt the connection between my boots and a Turkish bath is a perfectly self-evident one to a logical mind, and yet I should be obliged to you if you would indicate it."

"The train of reasoning is not very obscure, Watson," said Holmes with a mischievous twinkle. "It belongs to the same elementary class of deduction which I should illustrate if I were to ask you who shared your cab in your drive this morning."

"I don't admit that a fresh illustration is an explanation," said I with some asperity.

"Bravo, Watson! A very dignified and logical remonstrance. Let me see, what were the points? Take the last one first--the cab. You observe that you have some splashes on the left sleeve and shoulder of your coat. Had you sat in the centre of a hansom you would probably have had no splashes, and if you had they would certainly have been symmetrical. Therefore, it is clear that you sat at the side. Therefore, it is equally clear that you had a companion."

"That is very evident."

"Absurdly commonplace, is it not?"

"But the boots and the bath?"

"Equally childish. You are in the habit of doing up your boots in a certain way. I see them on this occasion fastened with an elaborate double bow, which is not your usual method of tying them. You have, therefore, had them off. Who has tied them? A bootmaker--or the boy at the bath. It is unlikely that it is the bootmaker, since your boots are nearly new. Well, what remains? The bath. Absurd, is it not? But, for all that, the Turkish bath has served a purpose."

"What is that?"

"You say that you have had it because you need a change. Let me suggest that you take one. How would Lausanne do, my dear Watson--first-class tickets and all expenses paid on a princely scale?"

"Splendid! But why?"

Holmes leaned back in his armchair and took his notebook from his pocket.

"One of the most dangerous classes in the world," said he, "is the drifting and friendless woman. She is the most harmless and often the most useful of mortals, but she is the inevitable inciter of crime in others. She is helpless. She is migratory. She has sufficient means to take her from country to country and from hotel to hotel. She is lost, as often as not, in a maze of obscure pensions and boardinghouses. She is a stray chicken in a world of foxes. When she is gobbled up she is hardly missed. I much fear that some evil has come to the Lady Frances Carfax."

I was relieved at this sudden descent from the general to the particular. Holmes consulted his notes.

"Lady Frances," he continued, "is the sole survivor of the direct family of the late Earl of Rufton. The estates went, as you may remember, in the male line. She was left with limited means, but with some very remarkable old Spanish jewellery of silver and curiously cut diamonds to which she was fondly attached--too attached, for she refused to leave them with her banker and always carried them about with her. A rather pathetic figure, the Lady Frances, a beautiful woman, still in fresh middle age, and yet, by a strange change, the last derelict of what only twenty years ago was a goodly fleet."

"What has happened to her, then?"

"Ah, what has happened to the Lady Frances? Is she alive or dead? There is our problem. She is a lady of precise habits, and for four years it has been her invariable custom to write every second week to Miss Dobney, her old governess, who has long retired and lives in Camberwell. It is this Miss Dobney who has consulted me. Nearly five weeks have passed without a word. The last letter was from the Hotel National at Lausanne. Lady Frances seems to have left there and given no address. The family are anxious, and as they are exceedingly wealthy no sum will be spared if we can clear the matter up."

"Is Miss Dobney the only source of information? Surely she had other correspondents?"

"There is one correspondent who is a sure draw, Watson. That is the bank. Single ladies must live, and their passbooks are compressed diaries. She banks at Silvester's. I have glanced over her account. The last check but one paid her bill at Lausanne, but it was a large one and probably left her with cash in hand. Only one check has been drawn since."

"To whom, and where?"

"To Miss Marie Devine. There is nothing to show where the check was drawn. It was cashed at the Credit Lyonnais at Montpellier less than three weeks ago. The sum was fifty pounds."

"And who is Miss Marie Devine?"

"That also I have been able to discover. Miss Marie Devine was the maid of Lady Frances Carfax. Why she should have paid her this check we have not yet determined. I have no doubt, however, that your researches will soon clear the matter up."

"MY researches!"

"Hence the health-giving expedition to Lausanne. You know that I cannot possibly leave London while old Abrahams is in such mortal terror of his life. Besides, on general principles it is best that I should not leave the country. Scotland Yard feels lonely without me, and it causes an unhealthy excitement among the criminal classes. Go, then, my dear Watson, and if my humble counsel can ever be valued at so extravagant a rate as two pence a word, it waits your disposal night and day at the end of the Continental wire."

Two days later found me at the Hotel National at Lausanne, where I received every courtesy at the hands of M. Moser, the well-known manager. Lady Frances, as he informed me, had stayed there for several weeks. She had been much liked by all who met her. Her age was not more than forty. She was still handsome and bore every sign of having in her youth been a very lovely woman. M. Moser knew nothing of any valuable jewellery, but it had been remarked by the servants that the heavy trunk in the lady's bedroom was always scrupulously locked. Marie Devine, the maid, was as popular as her mistress. She was actually engaged to one of the head waiters in the hotel, and there was no difficulty in getting her address. It was 11 Rue de Trajan, Montpellier. All this I jotted down and felt that Holmes himself could not have been more adroit in collecting his facts.

Only one corner still remained in the shadow. No light which I possessed could clear up the cause for the lady's sudden departure. She was very happy at Lausanne. There was every reason to believe that she intended to remain for the season in her luxurious rooms overlooking the lake. And yet she had left at a single day's notice, which involved her in the useless payment of a week's rent. Only Jules Vibart, the lover of the maid, had any suggestion to offer. He connected the sudden departure with the visit to the hotel a day or two before of a tall, dark, bearded man. "Un sauvage--un veritable sauvage!" cried Jules Vibart. The man had rooms somewhere in the town. He had been seen talking earnestly to Madame on the promenade by the lake. Then he had called. She had refused to see him. He was English, but of his name there was no record. Madame had left the place immediately afterwards. Jules Vibart and what was of more importance, Jules Vibart's sweetheart, thought that this call and the departure were cause and effect. Only one thing Jules would not discuss. That was the reason why Marie had left her mistress. Of that he could or would say nothing. If I wished to know, I must go to Montpellier and ask her.

So ended the first chapter of my inquiry. The second was devoted to the place which Lady Frances Carfax had sought when she left Lausanne. Concerning this there had been some secrecy, which confirmed the idea that she had gone with the intention of throwing someone off her track. Otherwise, why should not her luggage have been openly labelled for Baden? Both she and it reached the Rhenish spa by some circuitous route. This much I gathered from the manager of Cook's local office. So to Baden I went, after dispatching to Holmes an account of all my proceedings and receiving in reply a telegram of half-humorous commendation.

At Baden the track was not difficult to follow. Lady Frances had stayed at the Englischer Hof for a fortnight. While there she had made the acquaintance of a Dr. Shlessinger and his wife, a missionary from South America. Like most lonely ladies, Lady Frances found her comfort and occupation in religion. Dr. Shlessinger's remarkable personality, his wholehearted devotion and the fact that he was recovering from a disease contracted in the exercise of his apostolic duties affected her deeply. She had helped Mrs. Shlessinger in the nursing of the convalescent saint. He spent his day, as the manager described it to me, upon a lounge-chair on the veranda, with an attendant lady upon either side of him. He was preparing a map of the Holy Land, with special reference to the kingdom of the Midianites, upon which he was writing a monograph. Finally, having improved much in health, he and his wife had returned to London, and Lady Frances had started thither in their company. This was just three weeks before, and the manager had heard nothing since. As to the maid, Marie, she had gone off some days beforehand in floods of tears, after informing the other maids that she was leaving service forever. Dr. Shlessinger had paid the bill of the whole party before his departure.

"By the way," said the landlord in conclusion, "you are not the only friend of Lady Frances Carfax who is inquiring after her just now. Only a week or so ago we had a man here upon the same errand."

"Did he give a name?" I asked.

"None; but he was an Englishman, though of an unusual type."

"A savage?" said I, linking my facts after the fashion of my illustrious friend.

"Exactly. That describes him very well. He is a bulky, bearded, sunburned fellow, who looks as if he would be more at home in a farmers' inn than in a fashionable hotel. A hard, fierce man, I should think, and one whom I should be sorry to offend."

Already the mystery began to define itself, as figures grow clearer with the lifting of a fog. Here was this good and pious lady pursued from place to place by a sinister and unrelenting figure. She feared him, or she would not have fled from Lausanne. He had still followed. Sooner or later, he would overtake her. Had he already overtaken her? Was that the secret of her continued silence? Could the good people who were her companions not screen her from his violence or his blackmail? What horrible purpose, what deep design, lay behind this long pursuit? There was the problem which I had to solve.

To Holmes I wrote showing how rapidly and surely I had got down to the roots of the matter. In reply I had a telegram asking for a description of Dr. Shlessinger's left ear. Holmes's ideas of humour are strange and occasionally offensive, so I took no notice of his ill-timed jest--indeed, I had already reached Montpellier in my pursuit of the maid, Marie, before his message came.

I had no difficulty in finding the ex-servant and in learning all that she could tell me. She was a devoted creature, who had only left her mistress because she was sure that she was in good hands, and because her own approaching marriage made a separation inevitable in any case. Her mistress had, as she confessed with distress, shown some irritability of temper towards her during their stay in Baden, and had even questioned her once as if she had suspicions of her honesty, and this had made the parting easier than it would otherwise have been. Lady Frances had given her fifty pounds as a wedding-present. Like me, Marie viewed with deep distrust the stranger who had driven her mistress from Lausanne. With her own eyes she had seen him seize the lady's wrist with great violence on the public promenade by the lake. He was a fierce and terrible man. She believed that it was out of dread of him that Lady Frances had accepted the escort of the Shlessingers to London. She had never spoken to Marie about it, but many little signs had convinced the maid that her mistress lived in a state of continual nervous apprehension. So far she had got in her narrative, when suddenly she sprang from her chair and her face was convulsed with surprise and fear. "See!" she cried. "The miscreant follows still! There is the very man of whom I speak."

Through the open sitting-room window I saw a huge, swarthy man with a bristling black beard walking slowly down the centre of the street and staring eagerly at the numbers of the houses. It was clear that, like myself, he was on the track of the maid. Acting upon the impulse of the moment, I rushed out and accosted him.

"You are an Englishman," I said.

"What if I am?" he asked with a most villainous scowl.

"May I ask what your name is?"

"No, you may not," said he with decision.

The situation was awkward, but the most direct way is often the best.

"Where is the Lady Frances Carfax?" I asked.

He stared at me with amazement.

"What have you done with her? Why have you pursued her? I insist upon an answer!" said I.

The fellow gave a bellow of anger and sprang upon me like a tiger. I have held my own in many a struggle, but the man had a grip of iron and the fury of a fiend. His hand was on my throat and my senses were nearly gone before an unshaven French ouvrier in a blue blouse darted out from a cabaret opposite, with a cudgel in his hand, and struck my assailant a sharp crack over the forearm, which made him leave go his hold. He stood for an instant fuming with rage and uncertain whether he should not renew his attack. Then, with a snarl of anger, he left me and entered the cottage from which I had just come. I turned to thank my preserver, who stood beside me in the roadway.

"Well, Watson," said he, "a very pretty hash you have made of it! I rather think you had better come back with me to London by the night express."

An hour afterwards, Sherlock Holmes, in his usual garb and style, was seated in my private room at the hotel. His explanation of his sudden and opportune appearance was simplicity itself, for, finding that he could get away from London, he determined to head me off at the next obvious point of my travels. In the disguise of a workingman, he had sat in the cabaret waiting for my appearance.

"And a singularly consistent investigation you have made, my dear Watson," said he. "I cannot at the moment recall any possible blunder which you have omitted. The total effect of your proceeding has been to give the alarm everywhere and yet to discover nothing."

"Perhaps you would have done no better," I answered bitterly.

"There is no 'perhaps' about it. I have done better. Here is the Hon. Philip Green, who is a fellow-lodger with you in this hotel, and we may find him the starting-point for a more successful investigation."

A card had come up on a salver, and it was followed by the same bearded ruffian who had attacked me in the street. He started when he saw me.

"What is this, Mr. Holmes?" he asked. "I had your note, and I have come. But what has this man to do with the matter?"

"This is my old friend and associate, Dr. Watson, who is helping us in this affair."

The stranger held out a huge, sunburned hand, with a few words of apology.

"I hope I didn't harm you. When you accused me of hurting her I lost my grip of myself. Indeed, I'm not responsible in these days. My nerves are like live wires. But this situation is beyond me. What I want to know, in the first place, Mr. Holmes, is, how in the world you came to hear of my existence at all."

"I am in touch with Miss Dobney, Lady Frances's governess."

"Old Susan Dobney with the mob cap! I remember her well."

"And she remembers you. It was in the days before--before you found it better to go to South Africa."

"Ah, I see you know my whole story. I need hide nothing from you. I swear to you, Mr. Holmes, that there never was in this world a man who loved a woman with a more wholehearted love than I had for Frances. I was a wild youngster, I know--not worse than others of my class. But her mind was pure as snow. She could not bear a shadow of coarseness. So, when she came to hear of things that I had done, she would have no more to say to me. And yet she loved me--that is the wonder of it!--loved me well enough to remain single all her sainted days just for my sake alone. When the years had passed, and I had made my money at Barberton I thought perhaps I could seek her out and soften her. I had heard that she was still unmarried, I found her at Lausanne and tried all I knew. She weakened, I think, but her will was strong, and when next I called she had left the town. I traced her to Baden, and then after a time heard that her maid was here. I'm a rough fellow, fresh from a rough life, and when Dr. Watson spoke to me as he did I lost hold of myself for a moment. But for God's sake tell me what has become of the Lady Frances."

"That is for us to find out," said Sherlock Holmes with peculiar gravity. "What is your London address, Mr. Green?"

"The Langham Hotel will find me."

"Then may I recommend that you return there and be on hand in case I should want you? I have no desire to encourage false hopes, but you may rest assured that all that can be done will be done for the safety of Lady Frances. I can say no more for the instant. I will leave you this card so that you may be able to keep in touch with us. Now, Watson, if you will pack your bag I will cable to Mrs. Hudson to make one of her best efforts for two hungry travellers at 7:30 tomorrow."

A telegram was awaiting us when we reached our Baker Street rooms, which Holmes read with an exclamation of interest and threw across to me. "Jagged or torn," was the message and the place of origin, Baden.

"What is this?" I asked.

"It is everything," Holmes answered. "You may remember my seemingly irrelevant question as to this clerical gentleman's left ear. You did not answer it."

"I had left Baden and could not inquire."

"Exactly. For this reason, I sent a duplicate to the manager of the Englischer Hof, whose answer lies here."

"What does it show?"

"It shows, my dear Watson, that we are dealing with an exceptionally astute and dangerous man. The Rev. Dr. Shlessinger, missionary from South America, is none other than Holy Peters, one of the most unscrupulous rascals that Australia has ever evolved--and for a young country it has turned out some very finished types. His particular specialty is the beguiling of lonely ladies by playing upon their religious feelings, and his so-called wife, an Englishwoman named Fraser, is a worthy helpmate. The nature of his tactics suggested his identity to me, and this physical peculiarity--he was badly bitten in a saloon-fight at Adelaide in '89--confirmed my suspicion. This poor lady is in the hands of a most infernal couple, who will stick at nothing, Watson. That she is already dead is a very likely supposition. If not, she is undoubtedly in some sort of confinement and unable to write to Miss Dobney or her other friends. It is always possible that she never reached London, or that she has passed through it, but the former is improbable, as, with their system of registration, it is not easy for foreigners to play tricks with the Continental police; and the latter is also unlikely, as these rouges could not hope to find any other place where it would be as easy to keep a person under restraint. All my instincts tell me that she is in London, but as we have at present no possible means of telling where, we can only take the obvious steps, eat our dinner, and possess our souls in patience. Later in the evening I will stroll down and have a word with friend Lestrade at Scotland Yard."

But neither the official police nor Holmes's own small but very efficient organization sufficed to clear away the mystery. Amid the crowded millions of London, the three persons we sought were as completely obliterated as if they had never lived. Advertisements were tried and failed. Clues were followed and led to nothing. Every criminal resort which Shlessinger might frequent was drawn in vain. His old associates were watched, but they kept clear of him. And then suddenly, after a week of helpless suspense there came a flash of light. A silver-and-brilliant pendant of old Spanish design had been pawned at Bovington's, in Westminster Road. The pawner was a large, clean-shaven man of clerical appearance. His name and address were demonstrably false. The ear had escaped notice, but the description was surely that of Shlessinger.

Three times had our bearded friend from the Langham called for news--the third time within an hour of this fresh development. His clothes were getting looser on his great body. He seemed to be wilting away in his anxiety. "If you will only give me something to do!" was his constant wail. At last Holmes could oblige him.

"He has begun to pawn the jewels. We should get him now."

"But does this mean that any harm has befallen the Lady Frances?"

Holmes shook his head very gravely.

"Supposing that they have held her prisoner up to now, it is clear that they cannot let her loose without their own destruction. We must prepare for the worst."

"What can I do?"

"These people do not know you by sight?"

"No."

"It is possible that he will go to some other pawnbroker in the future. In that case, we must begin again. On the other hand, he has had a fair price, and no questions asked, so if he is in need of ready-money he will probably come back to Bovington's. I will give you a note to them, and they will let you wait in the shop. If the fellow comes you will follow him home. But no indiscretion, and, above all, no violence. I put you on your honour that you will take no step without my knowledge and consent."

For two days the Hon. Philip Green (he was, I may mention, the son of the famous admiral of that name who commanded the Sea of Azof fleet in the Crimean War) brought us no news. On the evening of the third he rushed into our sitting-room, pale, trembling, with every muscle of his powerful frame quivering with excitement.

"We have him! We have him!" he cried.

He was incoherent in his agitation. Holmes soothed him with a few words and thrust him into an armchair.

"Come, now, give us the order of events," said he.

"She came only an hour ago. It was the wife, this time, but the pendant she brought was the fellow of the other. She is a tall, pale woman, with ferret eyes."

"That is the lady," said Holmes.

"She left the office, and I followed her. She walked up the Kennington Road, and I kept behind her. Presently she went into a shop. Mr. Holmes, it was an undertaker's."

My companion started. "Well?" he asked in that vibrant voice which told of the fiery soul behind the cold gray face.

"She was talking to the woman behind the counter. I entered as well. 'It is late,' I heard her say, or words to that effect. The woman was excusing herself. 'It should be there before now,' she answered. 'It took longer, being out of the ordinary.' They both stopped and looked at me, so I asked some questions and then left the shop."

"You did excellently well. What happened next?"

"The woman came out, but I had hid myself in a doorway. Her suspicions had been aroused, I think, for she looked round her. Then she called a cab and got in. I was lucky enough to get another and so to follow her. She got down at last at No. 36, Poultney Square, Brixton. I drove past, left my cab at the corner of the square, and watched the house."

"Did you see anyone?"

"The windows were all in darkness save one on the lower floor. The blind was down, and I could not see in. I was standing there, wondering what I should do next, when a covered van drove up with two men in it. They descended, took something out of the van, and carried it up the steps to the hall door. Mr. Holmes, it was a coffin."

"Ah!"

"For an instant I was on the point of rushing in. The door had been opened to admit the men and their burden. It was the woman who had opened it. But as I stood there she caught a glimpse of me, and I think that she recognized me. I saw her start, and she hastily closed the door. I remembered my promise to you, and here I am."

"You have done excellent work," said Holmes, scribbling a few words upon a half-sheet of paper. "We can do nothing legal without a warrant, and you can serve the cause best by taking this note down to the authorities and getting one. There may be some difficulty, but I should think that the sale of the jewellery should be sufficient. Lestrade will see to all details."

"But they may murder her in the meanwhile. What could the coffin mean, and for whom could it be but for her?"

"We will do all that can be done, Mr. Green. Not a moment will be lost. Leave it in our hands. Now Watson," he added as our client hurried away, "he will set the regular forces on the move. We are, as usual, the irregulars, and we must take our own line of action. The situation strikes me as so desperate that the most extreme measures are justified. Not a moment is to be lost in getting to Poultney Square.

"Let us try to reconstruct the situation," said he as we drove swiftly past the Houses of Parliament and over Westminster Bridge. "These villains have coaxed this unhappy lady to London, after first alienating her from her faithful maid. If she has written any letters they have been intercepted. Through some confederate they have engaged a furnished house. Once inside it, they have made her a prisoner, and they have become possessed of the valuable jewellery which has been their object from the first. Already they have begun to sell part of it, which seems safe enough to them, since they have no reason to think that anyone is interested in the lady's fate. When she is released she will, of course, denounce them. Therefore, she must not be released. But they cannot keep her under lock and key forever. So, murder is their only solution."

"That seems very clear."

"Now we will take another line of reasoning. When you follow two separate chains of thought, Watson, you will find some point of intersection which should approximate to the truth. We will start now, not from the lady but from the coffin and argue backward. That incident proves, I fear, beyond all doubt that the lady is dead. It points also to an orthodox burial with proper accompaniment of medical certificate and official sanction. Had the lady been obviously murdered, they would have buried her in a hole in the back garden.

But here all is open and regular. What does this mean? Surely that they have done her to death in some way which has deceived the doctor and simulated a natural end--poisoning, perhaps. And yet how strange that they should ever let a doctor approach her unless he were a confederate, which is hardly a credible proposition."

"Could they have forged a medical certificate?"

"Dangerous, Watson, very dangerous. No, I hardly see them doing that. Pull up, cabby! This is evidently the undertakers, for we have just passed the pawnbrokers. Would you go in, Watson? Your appearance inspires confidence. Ask what hour the Poultney Square funeral takes place tomorrow."

The woman in the shop answered me without hesitation that it was to be at eight o'clock in the morning. "You see, Watson, no mystery; everything above-board! In some way the legal forms have undoubtedly been complied with, and they think that they have little to fear. Well, there's nothing for it now but a direct frontal attack. Are you armed?"

"My stick!"

"Well, well, we shall be strong enough. 'Thrice is he armed who hath his quarrel just.' We simply can't afford to wait for the police or to keep within the four corners of the law. You can drive off, cabby. Now, Watson, we'll just take our luck together, as we have occasionally in the past."

He had rung loudly at the door of a great dark house in the centre of Poultney Square. It was opened immediately, and the figure of a tall woman was outlined against the dim-lit hall.

"Well, what do you want?" she asked sharply, peering at us through the darkness.

"I want to speak to Dr. Shlessinger," said Holmes.

"There is no such person here," she answered, and tried to close the door, but Holmes had jammed it with his foot.

"Well, I want to see the man who lives here, whatever he may call himself," said Holmes firmly.

She hesitated. Then she threw open the door. "Well, come in!" said she. "My husband is not afraid to face any man in the world." She closed the door behind us and showed us into a sitting-room on the right side of the hall, turning up the gas as she left us. "Mr. Peters will be with you in an instant," she said.

Her words were literally true, for we had hardly time to look around the dusty and moth-eaten apartment in which we found ourselves before the door opened and a big, clean-shaven bald-headed man stepped lightly into the room. He had a large red face, with pendulous cheeks, and a general air of superficial benevolence which was marred by a cruel, vicious mouth.

"There is surely some mistake here, gentlemen," he said in an unctuous, make-everything-easy voice. "I fancy that you have been misdirected. Possibly if you tried farther down the street--"

"That will do; we have no time to waste," said my companion firmly. "You are Henry Peters, of Adelaide, late the Rev. Dr. Shlessinger, of Baden and South America. I am as sure of that as that my own name is Sherlock Holmes."

Peters, as I will now call him, started and stared hard at his formidable pursuer. "I guess your name does not frighten me, Mr. Holmes," said he coolly. "When a man's conscience is easy you can't rattle him. What is your business in my house?"

"I want to know what you have done with the Lady Frances Carfax, whom you brought away with you from Baden."

"I'd be very glad if you could tell me where that lady may be," Peters answered coolly. "I've a bill against her for nearly a hundred pounds, and nothing to show for it but a couple of trumpery pendants that the dealer would hardly look at. She attached herself to Mrs. Peters and me at Baden--it is a fact that I was using another name at the time--and she stuck on to us until we came to London. I paid her bill and her ticket. Once in London, she gave us the slip, and, as I say, left these out-of-date jewels to pay her bills. You find her, Mr. Holmes, and I'm your debtor."

"I mean to find her," said Sherlock Holmes. "I'm going through this house till I do find her."

"Where is your warrant?"

Holmes half drew a revolver from his pocket. "This will have to serve till a better one comes."

"Why, you're a common burglar."

"So, you might describe me," said Holmes cheerfully. "My companion is also a dangerous ruffian. And together we are going through your house."

Our opponent opened the door.

"Fetch a policeman, Annie!" said he. There was a whisk of feminine skirts down the passage, and the hall door was opened and shut.

"Our time is limited, Watson," said Holmes. "If you try to stop us, Peters, you will most certainly get hurt. Where is that coffin which was brought into your house?"

"What do you want with the coffin? It is in use. There is a body in it."

"I must see the body."

"Never with my consent."

"Then without it." With a quick movement Holmes pushed the fellow to one side and passed into the hall. A door half opened stood immediately before us. We entered. It was the dining-room. On the table, under a half-lit chandelier, the coffin was lying. Holmes turned up the gas and raised the lid. Deep down in the recesses of the coffin lay an emaciated figure. The glare from the lights above beat down upon an aged and withered face. By no possible process of cruelty, starvation or disease could this worn-out wreck be the still beautiful Lady Frances. Holmes's face showed his amazement, and also his relief.

"Thank God!" he muttered. "It's someone else."

"Ah, you've blundered badly for once, Mr. Sherlock Holmes," said Peters, who had followed us into the room.

"Who is the dead woman?"

"Well, if you really must know, she is an old nurse of my wife's, Rose Spender by name, whom we found in the Brixton Workhouse Infirmary. We brought her round here, called in Dr. Horsom, of 13 Firbank Villas--mind you take the address, Mr. Holmes--and had her carefully tended, as Christian folk should. On the third day she died--certificate says senile decay--but that's only the doctor's opinion, and of course you know better. We ordered her funeral to be carried out by Stimson and Co., of the Kennington Road, who will bury her at eight o'clock tomorrow morning. Can you pick any hole in that, Mr. Holmes? You've made a silly blunder, and you may as well own up to it. I'd give something for a photograph of your gaping, staring face when you pulled aside that lid expecting to see the Lady Frances Carfax and only found a poor old woman of ninety."

Holmes's expression was as impassive as ever under the jeers of his antagonist, but his clenched hands betrayed his acute annoyance.

"I am going through your house," said he.

"Are you, though!" cried Peters as a woman's voice and heavy steps sounded in the passage. "We'll soon see about that. This way, officers, if you please. These men have forced their way into my house, and I cannot get rid of them. Help me to put them out."

A sergeant and a constable stood in the doorway. Holmes drew his card from his case.

"This is my name and address. This is my friend, Dr. Watson."

"Bless you, sir, we know you very well," said the sergeant, "but you can't stay here without a warrant."

"Of course not. I quite understand that."

"Arrest him!" cried Peters.

"We know where to lay our hands on this gentleman if he is wanted," said the sergeant majestically, "but you'll have to go, Mr. Holmes."

"Yes, Watson, we shall have to go."

A minute later we were in the street once more. Holmes was as cool as ever, but I was hot with anger and humiliation. The sergeant had followed us.

"Sorry, Mr. Holmes, but that's the law."

"Exactly, Sergeant, you could not do otherwise."

"I expect there was good reason for your presence there. If there is anything I can do--"

"It's a missing lady, Sergeant, and we think she is in that house. I expect a warrant presently."

"Then I'll keep my eye on the parties, Mr. Holmes. If anything comes along, I will surely let you know."

It was only nine o'clock, and we were off full cry upon the trail at once. First we drove to Brixton Workhouse Infirmary, where we found that it was indeed the truth that a charitable couple had called some days before, that they had claimed an imbecile old woman as a former servant, and that they had obtained permission to take her away with them. No surprise was expressed at the news that she had since died.

The doctor was our next goal. He had been called in, had found the woman dying of pure senility, had actually seen her pass away, and had signed the certificate in due form. "I assure you that everything was perfectly normal and there was no room for foul play in the matter," said he. Nothing in the house had struck him as suspicious save that for people of their class it was remarkable that they should have no servant. So far and no further went the doctor.

Finally, we found our way to Scotland Yard. There had been difficulties of procedure in regard to the warrant. Some delay was inevitable. The magistrate's signature might not be obtained until next morning. If Holmes would call about nine he could go down with Lestrade and see it acted upon. So ended the day, save that near midnight our friend, the sergeant, called to say that he had seen flickering lights here and there in the windows of the great dark house, but that no one had left it, and none had entered. We could but pray for patience and wait for the morrow.

Sherlock Holmes was too irritable for conversation and too restless for sleep. I left him smoking hard, with his heavy, dark brows knotted together, and his long, nervous fingers tapping upon the arms of his chair, as he turned over in his mind every possible solution of the mystery. Several times in the course of the night I heard him prowling about the house. Finally, just after I had been called in the morning, he rushed into my room. He was in his dressing-gown, but his pale, hollow-eyed face told me that his night had been a sleepless one.

"What time was the funeral? Eight, was it not?" he asked eagerly. "Well, it is 7:20 now. Good heavens, Watson, what has become of any brains that God has given me? Quick, man, quick! It's life or death--a hundred chances on death to one on life. I'll never forgive myself, never, if we are too late!"

Five minutes had not passed before we were flying in a hansom down Baker Street. But even so it was twenty-five to eight as we passed Big Ben, and eight struck as we tore down the Brixton Road. But others were late as well as we. Ten minutes after the hour the hearse was still standing at the door of the house, and even as our foaming horse came to a halt the coffin, supported by three men, appeared on the threshold. Holmes darted forward and barred their way.

"Take it back!" he cried, laying his hand on the breast of the foremost. "Take it back this instant!"

"What the devil do you mean? Once again I ask you, where is your warrant?" shouted the furious Peters, his big red face glaring over the farther end of the coffin.

"The warrant is on its way. The coffin shall remain in the house until it comes."

The authority in Holmes's voice had its effect upon the bearers. Peters had suddenly vanished into the house, and they obeyed these new orders. "Quick, Watson, quick! Here is a screw-driver!" he shouted as the coffin was replaced upon the table. "Here's one for you, my man! A sovereign if the lid comes off in a minute! Ask no questions-- work away! That's good! Another! And another! Now pull all together! It's giving! It's giving! Ah, that does it at last."

With a united effort we tore off the coffin-lid. As we did so there came from the inside a stupefying and overpowering smell of chloroform. A body lay within, its head all wreathed in cotton-wool, which had been soaked in the narcotic. Holmes plucked it off and disclosed the statuesque face of a handsome and spiritual woman of middle age. In an instant he had passed his arm round the figure and raised her to a sitting position.

"Is she gone, Watson? Is there a spark left? Surely we are not too late!"

For half an hour it seemed that we were. What with actual suffocation, and what with the poisonous fumes of the chloroform, the Lady Frances seemed to have passed the last point of recall. And then, at last, with artificial respiration, with injected ether, and with every device that science could suggest, some flutter of life, some quiver of the eyelids, some dimming of a mirror, spoke of the slowly returning life. A cab had driven up, and Holmes, parting the blind, looked out at it. "Here is Lestrade with his warrant," said he. "He will find that his birds have flown. And here," he added as a heavy step hurried along the passage, "is someone who has a better right to nurse this lady than we have. Good morning, Mr. Green; I think that the sooner we can move the Lady Frances the better. Meanwhile, the funeral may proceed, and the poor old woman who still lies in that coffin may go to her last resting-place alone."

"Should you care to add the case to your annals, my dear Watson," said Holmes that evening, "it can only be as an example of that temporary eclipse to which even the best-balanced mind may be exposed. Such slips are common to all mortals, and the greatest is he who can recognize and repair them. To this modified credit I may, perhaps, make some claim. My night was haunted by the thought that somewhere a clue, a strange sentence, a curious observation, had come under my notice and had been too easily dismissed. Then, suddenly, in the gray of the morning, the words came back to me. It was the remark of the undertaker's wife, as reported by Philip Green. She had said, 'It should be there before now. It took longer, being out of the ordinary.' It was the coffin of which she spoke. It had been out of the ordinary. That could only mean that it had been made to some special measurement. But why? Why? Then in an instant I remembered the deep sides, and the little wasted figure at the bottom. Why so large a coffin for so small a body? To leave room for another body. Both would be buried under the one certificate. It had all been so clear, if only my own sight had not been dimmed. At eight the Lady Frances would be buried. Our one chance was to stop the coffin before it left the house.

"It was a desperate chance that we might find her alive, but it was a chance, as the result showed. These people had never, to my knowledge, done a murder. They might shrink from actual violence at the last. The could bury her with no sign of how she met her end, and even if she were exhumed there was a chance for them. I hoped that such considerations might prevail with them. You can reconstruct the scene well enough. You saw the horrible den upstairs, where the poor lady had been kept so long. They rushed in and overpowered her with their chloroform, carried her down, poured more into the coffin to insure against her waking, and then screwed down the lid. A clever device, Watson. It is new to me in the annals of crime. If our ex-missionary friends escape the clutches of Lestrade, I shall expect to hear of some brilliant incidents in their future career."

THE BEETLE-HUNTER

A curious experience? said the Doctor. Yes, my friends, I have had one very curious experience. I never expect to have another, for it is against all doctrines of chances that two such events would befall any one man in a single lifetime. You may believe me or not, but the thing happened exactly as I tell it.

I had just become a medical man, but I had not started in practice, and I lived in rooms in Gower Street. The street has been renumbered since then, but it was in the only house which has a bow-window, upon the left-hand side as you go down from the Metropolitan Station. A widow named Murchison kept the house at that time, and she had three medical students and one engineer as lodgers. I occupied the top room, which was the cheapest, but cheap as it was it was more than I could afford. My small resources were dwindling away, and every week it became more necessary that I should find something to do. Yet I was very unwilling to go into general practice, for my tastes were all in the direction of science, and especially of zoology, towards which I had always a strong leaning. I had almost given the fight up and resigned myself to being a medical drudge for life, when the turning-point of my struggles came in a very extraordinary way.

One morning I had picked up the Standard and was glancing over its contents. There was a complete absence of news, and I was about to toss the paper down again, when my eyes were caught by an advertisement at the head of the personal column. It was worded in this way:

"Wanted for one or more days the services of a medical man. It is essential that he should be a man of strong physique, of steady nerves, and of a resolute nature. Must be an entomologist—coleopterist preferred. Apply, in person, at 77B, Brook Street. Application must be made before twelve o'clock today."

Now, I have already said that I was devoted to zoology. Of all branches of zoology, the study of insects was the most attractive to me, and of all insects' beetles were the species with which I was most familiar. Butterfly collectors are numerous, but beetles are far more varied, and more accessible in these islands than are butterflies. It was this fact which had attracted my attention to them, and I had myself made a collection which numbered some hundred varieties. As to the other requisites of the advertisement, I knew that my nerves could be depended upon, and I had won the weight-throwing competition at the inter-hospital sports. Clearly, I was the very man for the vacancy. Within five minutes of my having read the advertisement I was in a cab and on my was to Brook Street.

As I drove, I kept turning the matter over in my head and trying to make a guess as to what sort of employment it could be which needed such curious qualifications. A strong physique, a resolute nature, a medical training, and a knowledge of beetles—what connection could there be between these various requisites? And then there was the disheartening fact that the situation was not a permanent one, but terminable from day to day, according to the terms of the advertisement. The more I pondered over it the more unintelligible did it become; but at the end of my meditations, I always came back to the ground fact that, come what might, I had nothing to lose, that I was completely at the end of my resources, and that I was ready for any adventure, however desperate, which would put a few honest sovereigns into my pocket. The man fears to fail who has to pay for his failure, but there was no penalty which Fortune could exact from me. I was like the gambler with empty pockets, who is still allowed to try his luck with the others.

No. 77B, Brook Street, was one of those dingy and yet imposing houses, dun-coloured and flat-faced, with the intensely respectable and solid air which marks the Georgian builder. As I alighted from the cab, a young man came out of the door and walked swiftly down the street. In passing me, I noticed that he cast an inquisitive and somewhat malevolent glance at me, and I took the incident as a good omen, for his appearance was that of a rejected candidate, and if he resented my application it meant that the vacancy was not yet filled up. Full of hope, I ascended the broad steps and rapped with the heavy knocker.

A footman in powder and livery opened the door. Clearly I was in touch with the people of wealth and fashion.

"Yes, sir?" said the footman.

"I came in answer to———"

"Quite so, sir," said the footman. "Lord Linchmere will see you at once in the library."

Lord Linchmere! I had vaguely heard the name but could not for the instant recall anything about him. Following the footman, I was shown into a large, book-lined room in which there was seated behind a writing-desk a small man with a pleasant, clean-shaven, mobile face, and long hair shot with grey, brushed back from his forehead. He looked me up and down with a very shrewd, penetrating glance, holding the card which the footman had given him in his right hand. Then he smiled pleasantly, and I felt that externally at any rate I possessed the qualifications which he desired.

"You have come in answer to my advertisement, Dr. Hamilton?" he asked.

"Yes, sir."

"Do you fulfil the conditions which are there laid down?"

"I believe that I do."

"You are a powerful man, or so I should judge from your appearance.

"I think that I am fairly strong."

"And resolute?"

"I believe so."

"Have you ever known what it was to be exposed to imminent danger?"

"No, I don't know that I ever have."

"But you think you would be prompt and cool at such a time?"

"I hope so."

"Well, I believe that you would. I have the more confidence in you because you do not pretend to be certain as to what you would do in a position that was new to you. My impression is that, so far as personal qualities go, you are the very man of whom I am in search. That being settled, we may pass on to the next point."

"Which is?"

"To talk to me about beetles."

I looked across to see if he was joking, but, on the contrary, he was leaning eagerly forward across his desk, and there was an expression of something like anxiety in his eyes.

"I am afraid that you do not know about beetles," he cried.

"On the contrary, sir, it is the one scientific subject about which I feel that I really do know something."

"I am overjoyed to hear it. Please talk to me about beetles."

I talked. I do not profess to have said anything original upon the subject, but I gave a short sketch of the characteristics of the beetle, and ran over the more common species, with some allusions to the specimens in my own little collection and to the article upon "Burying Beetles" which I had contributed to the Journal of Entomological Science.

"What! not a collector?" cried Lord Linchmere. "You don't mean that you are yourself a collector?" His eyes danced with pleasure at the thought.

"You are certainly the very man in London for my purpose. I thought that among five millions of people there must be such a man, but the difficulty is to lay one's hands upon him. I have been extraordinarily fortunate in finding you."

He rang a gong upon the table, and the footman entered.

"Ask Lady Rossiter to have the goodness to step this way," said his lordship, and a few moments later the lady was ushered into the room. She was a small, middle-aged woman, very like Lord Linchmere in appearance, with the same quick, alert features and grey-black hair. The expression of anxiety, however, which I had observed upon his face was very much more marked upon hers. Some great grief seemed to have cast its shadow over her features. As Lord Linchmere presented me she turned her face full upon me, and I was shocked to observe a half-healed scar extending for two inches over her right eyebrow. It was partly concealed by plaster, but none the less I could see that it had been a serious wound and not long inflicted.

"Dr. Hamilton is the very man for our purpose, Evelyn," said Lord Linchmere. "He is actually a collector of beetles, and he has written articles upon the subject."

"Really!" said Lady Rossiter. "Then you must have heard of my husband. Everyone who knows anything about beetles must have heard of Sir Thomas Rossiter."

For the first time a thin little ray of light began to break into the obscure business. Here, at last, was a connection between these people and beetles. Sir Thomas Rossiter—he was the greatest authority upon the subject in the world. He had made it his lifelong study and had written a most exhaustive work upon it. I hastened to assure her that I had read and appreciated it.

"Have you met my husband?" she asked.

"No, I have not."

"But you shall," said Lord Linchmere, with decision.

The lady was standing beside the desk, and she put her hand upon his shoulder. It was obvious to me as I saw their faces together that they were brother and sister.

"Are you really prepared for this, Charles? It is noble of you, but you fill me with fears." Her voice quavered with apprehension, and he appeared to me to be equally moved, though he was making strong efforts to conceal his agitation.

"Yes, yes, dear; it is all settled, it is all decided; in fact, there is no other possible way, that I can see."

"There is one obvious way."

"No, no, Evelyn, I shall never abandon you—never. It will come right—depend upon it; it will come right, and surely it looks like the interference of Providence that so perfect an instrument should be put into our hands."

My position was embarrassing, for I felt that for the instant they had forgotten my presence. But Lord Linchmere came back suddenly to me and to my engagement.

"The business for which I want you, Dr. Hamilton, is that you should put yourself absolutely at my disposal. I wish you to come for a short journey with me, to remain always at my side, and to promise to do without question whatever I may ask you, however unreasonable it may appear to you to be."

"That is a good deal to ask," said I.

"Unfortunately, I cannot put it more plainly, for I do not myself know what turn matters may take. You may be sure, however, that you will not be asked to do anything which your conscience does not approve; and I promise you that, when all is over, you will be proud to have been concerned in so good at work."

"If it ends happily," said the lady.

"Exactly; if it ends happily," his lordship repeated.

"And terms?" I asked.

"Twenty pounds a day."

I was amazed at the sum and must have showed my surprise upon my features.

"It is a rare combination of qualities, as must have struck you when you first read the advertisement," said Lord Linchmere; "such varied gifts may well command a high return, and I do not conceal from you that your duties might be arduous or even dangerous. Besides, it is possible that one or two days may bring the matter to an end."

"Please God!" sighed his sister.

"So now, Dr. Hamilton, may I rely upon your aid?"

"Most undoubtedly," said I. "You have only to tell me what my duties are."

"Your first duty will be to return to your home. You will pack up whatever you may need for a short visit to the country. We start together from Paddington Station at 3:40 this afternoon."

"Do we go far?"

"As far as Pangbourne. Meet me at the bookstall at 3:30. I shall have the tickets. Goodbye, Dr. Hamilton! And, by the way, there are two things which I should be very glad if you would bring with you, in case you have them. One is your case for collecting beetles, and the other is a stick, and the thicker and heavier the better."

You may imagine that I had plenty to think of from the time that I left Brook Street until I set out to meet Lord Linchmere at Paddington. The whole fantastic business kept arranging and rearranging itself in kaleidoscopic forms inside my brain, until I had thought out a dozen explanations, each of them more grotesquely improbable than the last. And yet I felt that the truth must be something grotesquely improbable also. At last, I gave up all attempts at finding a solution and contented myself with exactly carrying out the instructions which I had received. With a hand valise, specimen-case, and a loaded cane, I was waiting at the Paddington bookstall when Lord Linchmere arrived. He was an even smaller man than I had thought—frail and peaky, with a manner which was more nervous than it had been in the morning. He wore a long, thick travelling ulster, and I observed that he carried a heavy blackthorn cudgel in his hand.

"I have the tickets," said he, leading the way up the platform.

"This is our train. I have engaged a carriage, for I am particularly anxious to impress one or two things upon you while we travel down."

And yet all that he had to impress upon me might have been said in a sentence, for it was that I was to remember that I was there as a protection to himself, and that I was not on any consideration to leave him for an instant. This he repeated again and again as our journey drew to a close, with an insistence which showed that his nerves were thoroughly shaken.

"Yes," he said at last, in answer to my looks rather than to my words, "I am nervous, Dr. Hamilton. I have always been a timid man, and my timidity depends upon my frail physical health. But my soul is firm, and I can bring myself up to face a danger which a less-nervous man might shrink from. What I am doing now is done from no compulsion, but entirely from a sense of duty, and yet it is, beyond doubt, a desperate risk. If things should go wrong, I will have some claims to the title of martyr."

This eternal reading of riddles was too much for me. I felt that I must put a term to it.

"I think it would very much better, sir, if you were to trust me entirely," said I. "It is impossible for me to act effectively, when I do not know what are the objects which we have in view, or even where we are going."

"Oh, as to where we are going, there need be no mystery about that," said he; "we are going to Delamere Court, the residence of Sir Thomas Rossiter, with whose work you are so conversant. As to the exact object of our visit, I do not know that at this stage of the proceedings anything would be gained, Dr. Hamilton, by taking you into my complete confidence. I may tell you that we are acting—I say 'we,' because my sister, Lady Rossiter, takes the same view as myself—with the one object of preventing anything in the nature of a family scandal. That being so, you can understand that I am loath to give any explanations which are not absolutely necessary. It would be a different matter, Dr. Hamilton, if I were asking your advice. As matters stand, it is only your active help which I need, and I will indicate to you from time to time how you can best give it."

There was nothing more to be said, and a poor man can put up with a good deal for twenty pounds a day, but I felt none the less that Lord Linchmere was acting rather scurvily towards me. He wished to convert me into a passive tool, like the blackthorn in his hand. With his sensitive disposition I could imagine, however, that scandal would be abhorrent to him, and I realized that he would not take me into his confidence until no other course was open to him. I must trust to my own eyes and ears to solve the mystery, but I had every confidence that I should not trust to them in vain.

Delamere Court lies a good five miles from Pangbourne Station, and we drove for that distance in an open fly. Lord Linchmere sat in deep thought during the time, and he never opened his mouth until we were close to our destination. When he did speak it was to give me a piece of information which surprised me.

"Perhaps you are not aware," said he, "that I am a medical man like yourself?"

"No, sir, I did not know it."

"Yes, I qualified in my younger days, when there were several lives between me and the peerage. I have not had occasion to practise, but I have found it a useful education, all the same. I never regretted the years which I devoted to medical study. These are the gates of Delamere Court."

We had come to two high pillars crowned with heraldic monsters which flanked the opening of a winding avenue. Over the laurel bushes and rhododendrons, I could see a long, many-gabled mansion, girdled with ivy, and toned to the warm, cheery, mellow glow of old brick-work. My eyes were still fixed in admiration upon this delightful house when my companion plucked nervously at my sleeve.

"Here's Sir Thomas," he whispered. "Please talk beetle all you can."

A tall, thin figure, curiously angular and bony, had emerged through a gap in the hedge of laurels. In his hand he held a spud, and he wore gauntleted gardener's gloves. A broad-brimmed, grey hat cast his face into shadow, but it struck me as exceedingly austere, with an ill-nourished beard and harsh, irregular features. The fly pulled up and Lord Linchmere sprang out.

"My dear Thomas, how are you?" said he, heartily.

But the heartiness was by no means reciprocal. The owner of the grounds glared at me over his brother-in-law's shoulder, and I caught broken scraps of sentences—"well-known wishes ... hatred of strangers ... unjustifiable intrusion ... perfectly inexcusable." Then there was a muttered explanation, and the two of them came over together to the side of the fly.

"Let me present you to Sir Thomas Rossiter, Dr. Hamilton," said Lord Linchmere. "You will find that you have a strong community of tastes."

I bowed. Sir Thomas stood very stiffly, looking at me severely from under the broad brim of his hat.

"Lord Linchmere tells me that you know something about beetles," said he. "What do you know about beetles?"

"I know what I have learned from your work upon the coleoptera, Sir Thomas," I answered.

"Give me the names of the better-known species of the British scarabaei," said he.

I had not expected an examination, but fortunately I was ready for one. My answers seemed to please him, for his stern features relaxed.

"You appear to have read my book with some profit, sir," said he. "It is a rare thing for me to meet anyone who takes an intelligent interest in such matters. People can find time for such trivialities as sport or society, and yet the beetles are overlooked. I can assure you that the greater part of the idiots in this part of the country are unaware that I have ever written a book at all——I, the first man who ever described the true function of the elytra. I am glad to see you, sir, and I have no doubt that I can show you some specimens which will interest you." He stepped into the fly and drove up with us to the house, expounding to me as we went some recent researches which he had made into the anatomy of the lady-bird.

I have said that Sir Thomas Rossiter wore a large hat drawn down over his brows. As he entered the hall he uncovered himself, and I was at once aware of a singular characteristic which the hat had concealed. His forehead, which was naturally high, and higher still on account of receding hair, was in a continual state of movement. Some nervous weakness kept the muscles in a constant spasm, which sometimes produced a mere twitching and sometimes a curious rotary movement unlike anything which I had ever seen before. It was strikingly visible as he turned towards us after entering the study and seemed the more singular from the contrast with the hard, steady, grey eyes which looked out from underneath those palpitating brows.

"I am sorry," said he, "that Lady Rossiter is not here to help me to welcome you. By the way, Charles, did Evelyn say anything about the date of her return?"

"She wished to stay in town for a few more days," said Lord Linchmere. "You know how ladies' social duties accumulate if they have been for some time in the country. My sister has many old friends in London at present."

"Well, she is her own mistress, and I should not wish to alter her plans, but I shall be glad when I see her again. It is very lonely here without her company."

"I was afraid that you might find it so, and that was partly why I ran down. My young friend, Dr. Hamilton, is so much interested in the subject which you have made your own, that I thought you would not mind his accompanying me."

"I lead a retired life, Dr. Hamilton, and my aversion to strangers grows upon me," said our host. "I have sometimes thought that my nerves are not so good as they were. My travels in search of beetles in my younger days took me into many malarious and unhealthy places. But a brother coleopterist like yourself is always a welcome guest, and I shall be delighted if you will look over my collection, which I think that I may without exaggeration describe as the best in Europe."

And so, no doubt it was. He had a huge, oaken cabinet arranged in shallow drawers, and here, neatly ticketed and classified, were beetles from every corner of the earth, black, brown, blue, green, and mottled. Every now and then as he swept his hand over the lines and lines of impaled insects he would catch up some rare specimen, and, handling it with as much delicacy and reverence as if it were a precious relic, he would hold forth upon its peculiarities and the circumstances under which it came into his possession. It was evidently an unusual thing for him to meet with a sympathetic listener, and he talked and talked until the spring evening had deepened into night, and the gong announced that it was time to dress for dinner. All the time Lord Linchmere said nothing, but he stood at his brother-in-law's elbow, and I caught him continually shooting curious little, questioning glances into his face. And his own features expressed some strong emotion, apprehension, sympathy, expectation: I seemed to read them all. I was sure that Lord Linchmere was fearing something and awaiting something, but what that something might be I could not imagine.

The evening passed quietly but pleasantly, and I should have been entirely at my ease if it had not been for that continual sense of tension upon the part of Lord Linchmere. As to our host, I found that he improved upon acquaintance. He spoke constantly with affection of his absent wife, and also of his little son, who had recently been sent to school. The house, he said, was not the same without them. If it were not for his scientific studies, he did not know how he could get through the days. After dinner we smoked for some time in the billiard-room, and finally went early to bed.

And then it was that, for the first time, the suspicion that Lord Linchmere was a lunatic crossed my mind. He followed me into my bedroom, when our host had retired.

"Doctor," said he, speaking in a low, hurried voice, "you must come with me. You must spend the night in my bedroom."

"What do you mean?"

"I prefer not to explain. But this is part of your duties. My room is close by, and you can return to your own before the servant calls you in the morning."

"But why?" I asked.

"Because I am nervous of being alone," said he. "That's the reason, since you must have a reason."

It seemed rank lunacy, but the argument of those twenty pounds would overcome many objections. I followed him to his room.

"Well," said I, "there's only room for one in that bed."

"Only one shall occupy it," said he.

"And the other?"

"Must remain on watch."

"Why?" said I. "One would think you expected to be attacked."

"Perhaps I do."

"In that case, why not lock your door?"

"Perhaps I WANT to be attacked."

It looked more and more like lunacy. However, there was nothing for it but to submit. I shrugged my shoulders and sat down in the arm-chair beside the empty fireplace.

"I am to remain on watch, then?" said I, ruefully.

"We will divide the night. If you will watch until two, I will watch the remainder."

"Very good."

"Call me at two o'clock, then."

"I will do so."

"Keep your ears open, and if you hear any sounds wake me instantly—instantly, you hear?"

"You can rely upon it." I tried to look as solemn as he did.

"And for God's sake don't go to sleep," said he, and so, taking off only his coat, he threw the coverlet over him and settled down for the night.

It was a melancholy vigil and made more so by my own sense of its folly. Supposing that by any chance Lord Linchmere had cause to suspect that he was subject to danger in the house of Sir Thomas Rossiter, why on earth could he not lock his door and so protect himself? His own answer that he might wish to be attacked was absurd. Why should he possibly wish to be attacked? And who would wish to attack him? Clearly, Lord Linchmere was suffering from some singular delusion, and the result was that on an imbecile pretext I was to be deprived of my night's rest. Still, however absurd, I was determined to carry out his injunctions to the letter as long as I was in his employment. I sat, therefore, beside the empty fireplace, and listened to a sonorous chiming clock somewhere down the passage which gurgled and struck every quarter of an hour. It was an endless vigil. Save for that single clock, an absolute silence reigned throughout the great house. A small lamp stood on the table at my elbow, throwing a circle of light round my chair, but leaving the corners of the room draped in shadow. On the bed Lord Linchmere was breathing peacefully. I envied him his quiet sleep, and again and again my own eyelids drooped, but every time my sense of duty came to my help, and I sat up, rubbing my eyes and pinching myself with a determination to see my irrational watch to an end.

And I did so. From down the passage came the chimes of two o'clock, and I laid my hand upon the shoulder of the sleeper. Instantly he was sitting up, with an expression of the keenest interest upon his face.

"You have heard something?"

"No, sir. It is two o'clock."

"Very good. I will watch. You can go to sleep."

I lay down under the coverlet as he had done and was soon unconscious. My last recollection was of that circle of lamplight, and of the small, hunched-up figure and strained, anxious face of Lord Linchmere in the centre of it.

How long I slept I do not know; but I was suddenly aroused by a sharp tug at my sleeve. The room was in darkness, but a hot smell of oil told me that the lamp had only that instant been extinguished.

"Quick! Quick!" said Lord Linchmere's voice in my ear.

I sprang out of bed, he still dragging at my arm.

"Over here!" he whispered and pulled me into a corner of the room. "Hush! Listen!"

In the silence of the night, I could distinctly hear that someone was coming down the corridor. It was a stealthy step, faint and intermittent, as of a man who paused cautiously after every stride. Sometimes for half a minute there was no sound, and then came the shuffle and creak which told of a fresh advance. My companion was trembling with excitement. His hand, which still held my sleeve, twitched like a branch in the wind.

"What is it?" I whispered.

"It's he!"

"Sir Thomas?"

"Yes."

"What does he want?"

"Hush! Do nothing until I tell you."

I was conscious now that someone was trying the door. There was the faintest little rattle from the handle, and then I dimly saw a thin slit of subdued light. There was a lamp burning somewhere far down the passage, and it just sufficed to make the outside visible from the darkness of our room. The greyish slit grew broader and broader, very gradually, very gently, and then outlined against it I saw the dark figure of a man. He was squat and crouching, with the silhouette of a bulky and misshapen dwarf. Slowly the door swung open with this ominous shape framed in the centre of it. And then, in an instant, the crouching figure shot up, there was a tiger spring across the room and thud, thud, thud, came three tremendous blows from some heavy object upon the bed.

I was so paralysed with amazement that I stood motionless and staring until I was aroused by a yell for help from my companion. The open door shed enough light for me to see the outline of things, and there was little Lord Linchmere with his arms round the neck of his brother-in-law, holding bravely on to him like a game bull-terrier with its teeth into a gaunt deerhound. The tall, bony man dashed himself about, writhing round and round to get a grip upon his assailant; but the other, clutching on from behind, still kept his hold, though his shrill, frightened cries showed how unequal he felt the contest to be. I sprang to the rescue, and the two of us managed to throw Sir Thomas to the ground, though he made his teeth meet in my shoulder. With all my youth and weight and strength, it was a desperate struggle before we could master his frenzied struggles but at last, we secured his arms with the waist-cord of the dressing-gown which he was wearing. I was holding his legs while Lord Linchmere was endeavouring to relight the lamp, when there came the pattering of many feet in the passage, and the butler and two footmen, who had been alarmed by the cries, rushed into the room. With their aid we had no further difficulty in securing our prisoner, who lay foaming and glaring upon the ground. One glance at his face was enough to prove that he was a dangerous maniac, while the short, heavy hammer which lay beside the bed showed how murderous had been his intentions.

"Do not use any violence!" said Lord Linchmere, as we raised the struggling man to his feet. "He will have a period of stupor after this excitement. I believe that it is coming on already." As he spoke the convulsions became less violent, and the madman's head fell forward upon his breast, as if he were overcome by sleep. We led him down the passage and stretched him upon his own bed, where he lay unconscious, breathing heavily.

"Two of you will watch him," said Lord Linchmere. "And now, Dr. Hamilton, if you will return with me to my room, I will give you the explanation which my horror of scandal has perhaps caused me to delay too long. Come what may, you will never have cause to regret your share in this night's work.

"The case may be made clear in a very few words," he continued, when we were alone. "My poor brother-in-law is one of the best fellows upon earth, a loving husband and an estimable father, but he comes from a stock which is deeply tainted with insanity. He has more than once had homicidal outbreaks, which are the more painful because his inclination is always to attack the very person to whom he is most attached. His son was sent away to school to avoid this danger, and then came an attempt upon my sister, his wife, from which she escaped with injuries that you may have observed when you met her in London. You understand that he knows nothing of the matter when he is in his sound senses and would ridicule the suggestion that he could under any circumstances injure those whom he loves so dearly. It is often, as you know, a characteristic of such maladies that it is absolutely impossible to convince the man who suffers from them of their existence.

"Our great object was, of course, to get him under restraint before he could stain his hands with blood, but the matter was full of difficulty. He is a recluse in his habits and would not see any medical man. Besides, it was necessary for our purpose that the medical man should convince himself of his insanity; and he is sane as you or I, save on these very rare occasions. But, fortunately, before he has these attacks he always shows certain premonitory symptoms, which are providential danger-signals, warning us to be upon our guard. The chief of these is that nervous contortion of the forehead which you must have observed. This is a phenomenon which always appears from three to four days before his attacks of frenzy. The moment it showed itself his wife came into town on some pretext and took refuge in my house in Brook Street.

"It remained for me to convince a medical man of Sir Thomas's insanity, without which it was impossible to put him where he could do no harm. The first problem was how to get a medical man into his house. I bethought me of his interest in beetles, and his love for anyone who shared his tastes. I advertised, therefore, and was fortunate enough to find in you the very man I wanted. A stout companion was necessary, for I knew that the lunacy could only be proved by a murderous assault, and I had every reason to believe that that assault would be made upon myself, since he had the warmest regard for me in his moments of sanity. I think your intelligence will supply all the rest. I did not know that the attack would come by night, but I thought it very probable, for the crises of such cases usually do occur in the early hours of the morning. I am a very nervous man myself, but I saw no other way in which I could remove this terrible danger from my sister's life. I need not ask you whether you are willing to sign the lunacy papers."

"Undoubtedly. But two signatures are necessary."

"You forget that I am myself a holder of a medical degree. I have the papers on a side-table here, so if you will be good enough to sign them now, we can have the patient removed in the morning."

So that was my visit to Sir Thomas Rossiter, the famous beetle-hunter, and that was also my first step upon the ladder of success, for Lady Rossiter and Lord Linchmere have proved to be staunch friends, and they have never forgotten my association with them in the time of their need. Sir Thomas is out and said to be cured, but I still think that if I spent another night at Delamere Court, I should be inclined to lock my door upon the inside.

THE POT OF CAVIARE

It was the fourth day of the siege. Ammunition and provisions were both nearing an end. When the Boxer insurrection had suddenly flamed up, and roared, like a fire in dry grass, across Northern China, the few scattered Europeans in the outlying provinces had huddled together at the nearest defensible post and had held on for dear life until rescue came—or until it did not. In the latter case, the less said about their fate the better. In the former, they came back into the world of men with that upon their faces which told that they had looked very closely upon such an end as would ever haunt their dreams.

Ichau was only fifty miles from the coast, and there was a European squadron in the Gulf of Liantong. Therefore, the absurd little garrison, consisting of native Christians and railway men, with a German officer to command them and five civilian Europeans to support him, held on bravely with the conviction that help must soon come sweeping down to them from the low hills to eastward. The sea was visible from those hills and on the sea were their armed countrymen. Surely, then, they could not feel deserted. With brave hearts they manned the loopholes in the crumbling brick walls outlining the tiny European quarter, and they fired away briskly, if ineffectively, at the rapidly advancing sangars of the Boxers. It was certain that in another day or so they would be at the end of their resources, but then it was equally certain that in another day or so they must be relieved. It might be a little sooner or it might be a little later, but there was no one who ever ventured to hint that the relief would not arrive in time to pluck them out of the fire. Up to Tuesday night there was no word of discouragement.

It was true that on the Wednesday their robust faith in what was going forward behind those eastern hills had weakened a little. The grey slopes lay bare and unresponsive while the deadly sangars pushed ever nearer, so near that the dreadful faces which shrieked imprecations at them from time to time over the top could be seen in every hideous feature. There was not so much of that now since young Ainslie, of the Diplomatic service, with his neat little .303 sporting rifle, had settled down in the squat church tower, and had devoted his days to abating the nuisance. But a silent sangar is an even more impressive thing than a clamorous one, and steadily, irresistibly, inevitably, the lines of brick and rubble drew closer. Soon they would be so near that one rush would assuredly carry the frantic swordsmen over the frail entrenchment. It all seemed very black upon the Wednesday evening. Colonel Dresler, the German ex-infantry soldier, went about with an imperturbable face, but a heart of lead. Ralston, of the railway, was up half the night writing farewell letters. Professor Mercer, the old entomologist, was even more silent and grimly thoughtful than ever. Ainslie had lost some of his flippancy. On the whole, the ladies—Miss Sinclair, the nurse of the Scotch Mission, Mrs. Patterson, and her pretty daughter Jessie, were the most composed of the party. Father Pierre of the French Mission, was also unaffected, as was natural to one who regarded martyrdom as a glorious crown. The Boxers yelling for his blood beyond the walls disturbed him less than his forced association with the sturdy Scotch Presbyterian presence of Mr. Patterson, with whom for ten years he had wrangled over the souls of the natives. They passed each other now in the corridors as dog passes cat, and each kept a watchful eye upon the other lest even in the trenches he might filch some sheep from the rival fold, whispering heresy in his ear.

But the Wednesday night passed without a crisis, and on the Thursday all was bright once more. It was Ainslie up in the clock tower who had first heard the distant thud of a gun. Then Dresler heard it, and within half an hour it was audible to all—that strong iron voice, calling to them from afar and bidding them to be of good cheer, since help was coming. It was clear that the landing party from the squadron was well on its way. It would not arrive an hour too soon. The cartridges were nearly finished. Their half-rations of food would soon dwindle to an even more pitiful supply. But what need to worry about that now that relief was assured? There would be no attack that day, as most of the Boxers could be seen streaming off in the direction of the distant firing, and the long lines of sangars were silent and deserted. They were all able, therefore, to assemble at the lunch-table, a merry, talkative party, full of that joy of living which sparkles most brightly under the imminent shadow of death.

"The pot of caviare!" cried Ainslie. "Come, Professor, out with the pot of caviare!"

"Potz-tausend! yes," grunted old Dresler. "It is certainly time that we had that famous pot."

The ladies joined in, and from all parts of the long, ill-furnished table there came the demand for caviare.

It was a strange time to ask for such a delicacy, but the reason is soon told. Professor Mercer, the old Californian entomologist, had received a jar of caviare in a hamper of goods from San Francisco, arriving a day or two before the outbreak. In the general pooling and distribution of provisions this one dainty and three bottles of Lachryma Christi from the same hamper had been excepted and set aside. By common consent they were to be reserved for the final joyous meal when the end of their peril should be in sight. Even as they sat the thud-thud of the relieving guns came to their ears—more luxurious music to their lunch than the most sybaritic restaurant of London could have supplied. Before evening the relief would certainly be there. Why, then, should their stale bread not be glorified by the treasured caviare?

But the Professor shook his gnarled old head and smiled his inscrutable smile.

"Better wait," said he.

"Wait! Why wait?" cried the company.

"They have still far to come," he answered.

"They will be here for supper at the latest," said Ralston, of the railway—a keen, birdlike man, with bright eyes and long, projecting nose. "They cannot be more than ten miles from us now. If they only did two miles an hour it would make them due at seven."

"There is a battle on the way," remarked the Colonel. "You will grant two hours or three hours for the battle."

"Not half an hour," cried Ainslie. "They will walk through them as if they were not there. What can these rascals with their matchlocks and swords do against modern weapons?"

"It depends on who leads the column of relief," said Dresler. "If they are fortunate enough to have a German officer——"

"An Englishman for my money!" cried Ralston.

"The French commodore is said to be an excellent strategist," remarked Father Pierre.

"I don't see that it matters a toss," cried the exuberant Ainslie. "Mr. Mauser and Mr. Maxim are the two men who will see us through, and with them on our side no leader can go wrong. I tell you they will just brush them aside and walk through them. So now, Professor, come on with that pot of caviare!"

But the old scientist was unconvinced.

"We shall reserve it for supper," said he.

"After all," said Mr. Patterson, in his slow, precise Scottish intonation, "it will be a courtesy to our guests—the officers of the relief—if we have some palatable food to lay before them. I'm in agreement with the Professor that we reserve the caviare for supper."

The argument appealed to their sense of hospitality. There was something pleasantly chivalrous, too, in the idea of keeping their one little delicacy to give a savour to the meal of their preservers. There was no more talk of the caviare.

"By the way, Professor," said Mr. Patterson, "I've only heard today that this is the second time that you have been besieged in this way. I'm sure we should all be very interested to hear some details of your previous experience."

The old man's face set very grimly.

"I was in Sung-tong, in South China, in 'eighty-nine," said he.

"It's a very extraordinary coincidence that you should twice have been in such a perilous situation," said the missionary. "Tell us how you were relieved at Sung-tong."

The shadow deepened upon the weary face.

"We were not relieved," said he.

"What! the place fell?"

"Yes, it fell."

"And you came through alive?"

"I am a doctor as well as an entomologist. They had many wounded; they spared me."

"And the rest?"

"Assez! assez!" cried the little French priest, raising his hand in protest. He had been twenty years in China. The professor had said nothing, but there was something, some lurking horror, in his dull, grey eyes which had turned the ladies pale.

"I am sorry," said the missionary. "I can see that it is a painful subject. I should not have asked."

"No," the Professor answered, slowly. "It is wiser not to ask. It is better not to speak about such things at all. But surely those guns are very much nearer?"

There could be no doubt of it. After a silence the thud-thud had recommenced with a lively ripple of rifle-fire playing all round that deep bass master-note. It must be just at the farther side of the nearest hill. They pushed back their chairs and ran out to the ramparts. The silent-footed native servants came in and cleared the scanty remains from the table. But after they had left, the old Professor sat on there, his massive, grey-crowned head leaning upon his hands and the same pensive look of horror in his eyes. Some ghosts may be laid for years, but when they do rise it is not so easy to drive them back to their slumbers. The guns had ceased outside, but he had not observed it, lost as he was in the one supreme and terrible memory of his life.

His thoughts were interrupted at last by the entrance of the Commandant. There was a complacent smile upon his broad German face.

"The Kaiser will be pleased," said he, rubbing his hands. "Yes, certainly it should mean a decoration. 'Defence of Ichau against the Boxers by Colonel Dresler, late Major of the 114th Hanoverian Infantry.

Splendid resistance of small garrison against overwhelming odds.' It will certainly appear in the Berlin papers."

"Then you think we are saved?" said the old man, with neither emotion nor exultation in his voice.

The Colonel smiled.

"Why, Professor," said he, "I have seen you more excited on the morning when you brought back *Lepidus Mercerensis* in your collecting-box."

"The fly was safe in my collecting-box first," the entomologist answered. "I have seen so many strange turns of Fate in my long life that I do not grieve, nor do I rejoice until I know that I have cause. But tell me the news."

"Well," said the Colonel, lighting his long pipe, and stretching his gaitered legs in the bamboo chair, "I'll stake my military reputation that all is well. They are advancing swiftly, the firing has died down to show that resistance is at an end, and within an hour we'll see them over the brow. Ainslie is to fire his gun three times from the church tower as a signal, and then we shall make a little sally on our own account."

"And you are waiting for this signal?"

"Yes, we are waiting for Ainslie's shots. I thought I would spend the time with you, for I had something to ask you."

"What was it?"

"Well, you remember your talk about the other siege—the siege of Sung-tong. It interests me very much from a professional point of view. Now that the ladies and civilians are gone you will have no objection to discussing it."

"It is not a pleasant subject."

"No, I dare say not. Mein Gott! it was indeed a tragedy. But you have seen how I have conducted the defence here. Was it wise? Was it good? Was it worthy of the traditions of the German army?"

"I think you could have done no more."

"Thank you. But this other place, was it as ably defended? To me a comparison of this sort is very interesting. Could it have been saved?"

"No; everything possible was done—save only one thing."

"Ah! there was one omission. What was it?"

"No one—above all, no woman—should have been allowed to fall alive into the hands of the Chinese."

The Colonel held out his broad red hand and enfolded the long, white, nervous fingers of the Professor.

"You are right—a thousand times right. But do not think that this has escaped my thoughts. For myself I would die fighting, so would Ralston, so would Ainslie. I have talked to them, and it is settled. But the others, I have spoken with them, but what are you to do? There are the priest, and the missionary, and the women."

"Would they wish to be taken alive?"

"They would not promise to take steps to prevent it. They would not lay hands on their own lives. Their consciences would not permit it. Of course, it is all over now, and we need not speak of such dreadful things. But what would you have done in my place?"

"Kill them."

"Mein Gott! You would murder them?"

"In mercy I would kill them. Man, I have been through it. I have seen the death of the hot eggs; I have seen the death of the boiling kettle; I have seen the women—my God! I wonder that I have ever slept sound again." His usually impassive face was working and quivering with the agony of the remembrance. "I was strapped to a stake with thorns in my eyelids to keep them open, and my grief at their torture was a less thing than my self-reproach when I thought that I could with one tube of tasteless tablets have snatched them at the last instant from the hands of their tormentors. Murder! I am ready to stand at the Divine bar and answer for a thousand murders such as that! Sin! Why, it is such an act as might well cleanse the stain of real sin from the soul. But if, knowing what I do, I should have failed this second time to do it, then, by Heaven! there is no hell deep enough or hot enough to receive my guilty craven spirit."

The Colonel rose, and again his hand clasped that of the Professor.

"You speak sense," said he. "You are a brave, strong man, who know your own mind. Yes, by the Lord! you would have been my great help had things gone the other way. I have often thought and wondered in the dark, early hours of the morning, but I did not know how to do it. But we should have heard Ainslie's shots before now; I will go and see."

Again, the old scientist sat alone with his thoughts. Finally, as neither the guns of the relieving force nor yet the signal of their approach sounded upon his ears, he rose and was about to go himself upon the ramparts to make inquiry when the door flew open, and Colonel Dresler staggered into the room. His face was of a ghastly yellow-white, and his chest heaved like that of a man exhausted with running. There was brandy on the side-table, and he gulped down a glassful. Then he dropped heavily into a chair.

"Well," said the Professor, coldly, "they are not coming?"

"No, they cannot come."

There was silence for a minute or more, the two men staring blankly at each other.

"Do they all know?"

"No one knows but me."

"How did you learn?"

"I was at the wall near the postern gate—the little wooden gate that opens on the rose garden. I saw something crawling among the bushes. There was a knocking at the door. I opened it. It was a Christian Tartar, badly cut about with swords. He had come from the battle. Commodore Wyndham, the Englishman, had sent him. The relieving force had been checked. They had shot away most of their ammunition. They had entrenched themselves and sent back to the ships for more. Three days must pass before they could come. That was all. Mein Gott! it was enough."

The Professor bent his shaggy grey brows.

"Where is the man?" he asked.

"He is dead. He died of loss of blood. His body lies at the postern gate."

"And no one saw him?"

"Not to speak to."

"Oh! they did see him, then?"

"Ainslie must have seen him from the church tower. He must know that I have had tidings. He will want to know what they are. If I tell him they must all know."

"How long can we hold out?"

"An hour or two at the most."

"Is that absolutely certain?"

"I pledge my credit as a soldier upon it."

"Then we must fall?"

"Yes, we must fall."

"There is no hope for us?"

"None."

The door flew open and young Ainslie rushed in. Behind him crowded Ralston, Patterson, and a crowd of white men and of native Christians.

"You've had news, Colonel?"

Professor Mercer pushed to the front.

"Colonel Dresler has just been telling me. It is all right. They have halted but will be here in the early morning. There is no longer any danger."

A cheer broke from the group in the doorway. Everyone was laughing and shaking hands.

"But suppose they rush us before to-morrow morning?" cried Ralston, in a petulant voice. "What infernal fools these fellows are not to push on! Lazy devils, they should be court-martialled, every man of them."

"It's all safe," said Ainslie. "These fellows have had a bad knock. We can see their wounded being carried by the hundred over the hill. They must have lost heavily. They won't attack before morning."

"No, no," said the Colonel; "it is certain that they won't attack before morning. None the less, get back to your posts. We must give no point away." He left the room with the rest, but as he did so he looked back, and his eyes for an instant met those of the old Professor. "I leave it in your hands," was the message which he flashed. A stern set smile was his answer.

The afternoon wore away without the Boxers making their last attack. To Colonel Dresler it was clear that the unwonted stillness meant only that they were reassembling their forces from their fight with the relief column and were gathering themselves for the inevitable and final rush. To all the others it appeared that the siege was indeed over, and that the assailants had been crippled by the losses which they had already sustained. It was a joyous and noisy party, therefore, which met at the supper-table, when the three bottles of Lachryma Christi were uncorked and the famous port of caviare was finally opened. It was a large jar, and, though each had a tablespoonful of the delicacy, it was by no means exhausted. Ralston, who was an epicure, had a double allowance. He pecked away at it like a hungry bird. Ainslie, too, had a second helping. The Professor took a large spoonful himself, and Colonel Dresler, watching him narrowly, did the same. The ladies ate freely, save only pretty Miss Patterson, who disliked the salty, pungent taste. In spite of the hospitable entreaties of the Professor, her portion lay hardly touched at the side of her plate.

"You don't like my little delicacy. It is a disappointment to me when I had kept it for your pleasure," said the old man. "I beg that you will eat the caviare."

"I have never tasted it before. No doubt I should like it in time."

"Well, you must make a beginning. Why not start to educate your taste now? Do, please!"

Pretty Jessie Patterson's bright face shone with her sunny, boyish smile.

"Why, how earnest you are!" she laughed. "I had no idea you were so polite, Professor Mercer. Even if I do not eat it I am just as grateful."

"You are foolish not to eat it," said the Professor, with such intensity that the smile died from her face and her eyes reflected the earnestness of his own. "I tell you it is foolish not to eat caviare to-night."

"But why—why?" she asked.

"Because you have it on your plate. Because it is sinful to waste it."

"There! there!" said stout Mrs. Patterson, leaning across. "Don't trouble her anymore. I can see that she does not like it. But it shall not be wasted." She passed the blade of her knife under it and scraped it from Jessie's plate on to her own. "Now it won't be wasted. Your mind will be at ease, Professor."

But it did not seem at ease. On the contrary, his face was agitated like that of a man who encounters an unexpected and formidable obstacle. He was lost in thought.

The conversation buzzed cheerily. Everyone was full of his future plans.

"No, no, there is no holiday for me," said Father Pierre. "We priests don't get holidays. Now that the mission and school are formed I am to leave it to Father Amiel, and to push westwards to found another."

"You are leaving?" said Mr. Patterson. "You don't mean that you are going away from Ichau?"

Father Pierre shook his venerable head in waggish reproof. "You must not look so pleased, Mr. Patterson."

"Well, well, our views are very different," said the Presbyterian, "but there is no personal feeling towards you, Father Pierre. At the same time, how any reasonable educated man at this time of the world's history can teach these poor benighted heathen that——"

A general buzz of remonstrance silenced the theology.

"What will you do yourself, Mr. Patterson?" asked someone.

"Well, I'll take three months in Edinburgh to attend the annual meeting. You'll be glad to do some shopping in Princes Street, I'm thinking, Mary. And you, Jessie, you'll see some folk your own age. Then we can come back in the fall, when your nerves have had a rest."

"Indeed, we shall all need it," said Miss Sinclair, the mission nurse. "You know, this long strain takes me in the strangest way. At the present moment I can hear such a buzzing in my ears."

"Well, that's funny, for it's just the same with me," cried Ainslie. "An absurd up-and-down buzzing, as if a drunken bluebottle were trying experiments on his register. As you say, it must be due to nervous strain. For my part I am going back to Peking, and I hope I may get some promotion over this affair. I can get good polo here, and that's as fine a change of thought as I know. How about you, Ralston?"

"Oh, I don't know. I've hardly had time to think. I want to have a real good sunny, bright holiday and forget it all. It was funny to see all the letters in my room. It looked so black on Wednesday night that I had settled up my affairs and written to all my friends. I don't quite know how they were to be delivered, but I trusted to luck. I think I will keep those papers as a souvenir. They will always remind me of how close a shave we have had."

"Yes, I would keep them," said Dresler.

His voice was so deep and solemn that every eye was turned upon him.

"What is it, Colonel? You seem in the blues to-night." It was Ainslie who spoke.

"No, no; I am very contented."

"Well, so you should be when you see success in sight. I am sure we are all indebted to you for your science and skill. I don't think we could have held the place without you. Ladies and gentlemen, I ask you to drink the health of Colonel Dresler, of the Imperial German army. Er soll leben—hoch!"

They all stood up and raised their glasses to the soldier, with smiles and bows.

His pale face flushed with professional pride.

"I have always kept my books with me. I have forgotten nothing," said he. "I do not think that more could be done. If things had gone wrong with us and the place had fallen you would, I am sure, have freed me from any blame or responsibility." He looked wistfully round him.

"I'm voicing the sentiments of this company, Colonel Dresler," said the Scotch minister, "when I say——but Lord save us! what's amiss with Mr. Ralston?"

He had dropped his face upon his folded arms and was placidly sleeping.

"Don't mind him," said the Professor, hurriedly. "We are all in the stage of reaction now. I have no doubt that we are all liable to collapse. It is only to-night that we shall feel what we have gone through."

"I'm sure I can fully sympathize with him," said Mrs. Patterson. "I don't know when I have been sleepier. I can hardly hold my own head up." She cuddled back in her chair and shut her eyes.

"Well, I've never known Mary do that before," cried her husband, laughing heartily. "Gone to sleep over her supper! What ever will she think when we tell her of it afterwards? But the air does seem hot and heavy. I can certainly excuse anyone who falls asleep to-night. I think that I shall turn in early myself."

Ainslie was in a talkative, excited mood. He was on his feet once more with his glass in his hand.

"I think that we ought to have one drink all together, and then sing 'Auld Lang Syne,'" said he, smiling round at the company. "For a week we have all pulled in the same boat, and we've got to know each other as people never do in the quiet days of peace. We've learned to appreciate each other, and we've learned to appreciate each other's nations. There's the Colonel here stands for Germany. And Father Pierre is for France. Then there's the Professor for America. Ralston and I are Britishers. Then there's the ladies, God bless 'em! They have been angels of mercy and compassion all through the siege. I think we should drink the health of the ladies. Wonderful thing—the quiet courage, the patience, the—what shall I say?—the fortitude, the—the—by George, look at the Colonel! He's gone to sleep, too—most infernal sleepy weather." His glass crashed down upon the table, and he sank back, mumbling and muttering, into his seat. Miss Sinclair, the pale mission nurse, had dropped off also. She lay like a broken lily across the arm of her chair. Mr. Patterson looked round him and sprang to his feet. He passed his hand over his flushed forehead.

"This isn't natural, Jessie," he cried. "Why are they all asleep? There's Father Pierre—he's off too. Jessie, Jessie, your mother is cold. Is it sleep? Is it death? Open the windows! Help! help! help!" He staggered to his feet and rushed to the windows, but midway his head spun round, his knees sank under him, and he pitched forward upon his face.

The young girl had also sprung to her feet. She looked round her with horror-stricken eyes at her prostrate father and the silent ring of figures.

"Professor Mercer! What is it? What is it?" she cried. "Oh, my God, they are dying! They are dead!"

The old man had raised himself by a supreme effort of his will, though the darkness was already gathering thickly round him.

"My dear young lady," he said, stuttering and stumbling over the words, "we would have spared you this. It would have been painless to mind and body. It was cyanide. I had it in the caviare. But you would not have it."

"Great Heaven!" She shrank away from him with dilated eyes. "Oh, you monster! You monster! You have poisoned them!"

"No, no! I saved them. You don't know the Chinese. They are horrible. In another hour we should all have been in their hands. Take it now, child." Even as he spoke, a burst of firing broke out under the very windows of the room. "Hark! There they are! Quick, dear, quick, you may cheat them yet!" But his words fell upon deaf ears, for the girl had sunk back senseless in her chair. The old man stood listening for an instant to the firing outside. But what was that? Merciful Father, what was that? Was he going mad? Was it the effect of the drug? Surely it was a European cheer? Yes, there were sharp orders in English. There was the shouting of sailors. He could no longer doubt it. By some miracle the relief had come after all. He threw his long arms upwards in his despair. "What *have* I done? Oh, good Lord, what have I done?" he cried.

It was Commodore Wyndham himself who was the first, after his desperate and successful night attack, to burst into that terrible supper-room. Round the table sat the white and silent company. Only in the young girl who moaned and faintly stirred was any sign of 84life to be seen. And yet there was one in the circle who had the energy for a last supreme duty. The Commodore, standing stupefied at the door, saw a grey head slowly lifted from the table, and the tall form of the Professor staggered for an instant to its feet.

"Take care of the caviare! For God's sake, don't touch the caviare!" he croaked.

Then he sank back once more, and the circle of death was complete.

THE RING OF THOTH.

Mr. John Vansittart Smith, F.R.S., of 147-A Gower Street, was a man whose energy of purpose and clearness of thought might have placed him in the very first rank of scientific observers. He was the victim, however, of a universal ambition which prompted him to aim at distinction in many subjects rather than preeminence in one.

In his early days he had shown an aptitude for zoology and for botany which caused his friends to look upon him as a second Darwin, but when a professorship was almost within his reach he had suddenly discontinued his studies and turned his whole attention to chemistry. Here his researches upon the spectra of the metals had won him his fellowship in the Royal Society; but again, he played the coquette with his subject, and after a year's absence from the laboratory he joined the Oriental Society, and delivered a paper on the Hieroglyphic and Demotic inscriptions of El Kab, thus giving a crowning example both of the versatility and of the inconstancy of his talents.

The most fickle of wooers, however, is apt to be caught at last, and so it was with John Vansittart Smith. The more he burrowed his way into Egyptology the more impressed he became by the vast field which it opened to the inquirer, and by the extreme importance of a subject which promised to throw a light upon the first germs of human civilisation and the origin of the greater part of our arts and sciences. So struck was Mr. Smith that he straightway married an Egyptological young lady who had written upon the sixth dynasty, and having thus secured a sound base of operations he set himself to collect materials for a work which should unite the research of Lepsius and the ingenuity of Champollion. The preparation of this magnum opus entailed many hurried visits to the magnificent Egyptian collections of the Louvre, upon the last of which, no longer ago than the middle of last October, he became involved in a most strange and noteworthy adventure.

The trains had been slow, and the Channel had been rough, so that the student arrived in Paris in a somewhat befogged and feverish condition. On reaching the Hotel de France, in the Rue Laffitte, he had thrown himself upon a sofa for a couple of hours, but finding that he was unable to sleep, he determined, in spite of his fatigue, to make his way to the Louvre, settle the point which he had come to decide, and take the evening train back to Dieppe. Having come to this conclusion, he donned his greatcoat, for it was a raw rainy day, and made his way across the Boulevard des Italiens and down the Avenue de l'Opera. Once in the Louvre he was on familiar ground, and he speedily made his way to the collection of papyri which it was his intention to consult.

The warmest admirers of John Vansittart Smith could hardly claim for him that he was a handsome man. His high-beaked nose and prominent chin had something of the same acute and incisive character which distinguished his intellect. He held his head in a birdlike fashion, and birdlike, too, was the pecking motion with which, in conversation, he threw out his objections and retorts. As he stood, with the high collar of his greatcoat raised to his ears, he might have seen from the reflection in the glass-case before him that his appearance was a singular one. Yet it came upon him as a sudden jar when an English voice behind him exclaimed in very audible tones, "What a queer-looking mortal!"

The student had a large amount of petty vanity in his composition which manifested itself by an ostentatious and overdone disregard of all personal considerations. He straightened his lips and looked rigidly at the roll of papyrus, while his heart filled with bitterness against the whole race of travelling Britons.

"Yes," said another voice, "he really is an extraordinary fellow."

"Do you know," said the first speaker, "one could almost believe that by the continual contemplation of mummies the chap has become half a mummy himself?"

"He has certainly an Egyptian cast of countenance," said the other.

John Vansittart Smith spun round upon his heel with the intention of shaming his countrymen by a corrosive remark or two. To his surprise and relief, the two young fellows who had been conversing had their shoulders turned towards him and were gazing at one of the Louvre attendants who was polishing some brass-work at the other side of the room.

"Carter will be waiting for us at the Palais Royal," said one tourist to the other, glancing at his watch, and they clattered away, leaving the student to his labours.

"I wonder what these chatterers call an Egyptian cast of countenance," thought John Vansittart Smith, and he moved his position slightly in order to catch a glimpse of the man's face. He started as his eyes fell upon it. It was indeed the very face with which his studies had made him familiar. The regular statuesque features, broad brow, well-rounded chin, and dusky complexion were the exact counterpart of the innumerable statues, mummy-cases, and pictures which adorned the walls of the apartment.

The thing was beyond all coincidence. The man must be an Egyptian.

The national angularity of the shoulders and narrowness of the hips were alone sufficient to identify him.

John Vansittart Smith shuffled towards the attendant with some intention of addressing him. He was not light of touch in conversation and found it difficult to strike the happy mean between the brusqueness of the superior and the geniality of the equal. As he came nearer, the man presented his side face to him, but kept his gaze still bent upon his work. Vansittart Smith, fixing his eyes upon the fellow's skin, was conscious of a sudden impression that there was something inhuman and preternatural about its appearance. Over the temple and cheek-bone it was as glazed and as shiny as varnished parchment. There was no suggestion of pores. One could not fancy a drop of moisture upon that arid surface. From brow to chin, however, it was cross-hatched by a million delicate wrinkles, which shot and interlaced as though Nature in some Maori mood had tried how wild and intricate a pattern she could devise.

"Ou est la collection de Memphis?" asked the student, with the awkward air of a man who is devising a question merely for the purpose of opening a conversation.

"C'est la," replied the man brusquely, nodding his head at the other side of the room.

"Vous etes un Egyptien, n'est-ce pas?" asked the Englishman.

The attendant looked up and turned his strange dark eyes upon his questioner. They were vitreous, with a misty dry shininess, such as Smith had never seen in a human head before. As he gazed into them he saw some strong emotion gather in their depths, which rose and deepened until it broke into a look of something akin both to horror and to hatred.

"Non, monsieur; je suis Francais." The man turned abruptly and bent low over his polishing. The student gazed at him for a moment in astonishment, and then turning to a chair in a retired corner behind one of the doors he proceeded to make notes of his researches among the papyri. His thoughts, however refused to return into their natural groove. They would run upon the enigmatical attendant with the sphinx-like face and the parchment skin.

"Where have I seen such eyes?" said Vansittart Smith to himself. "There is something saurian about them, something reptilian. There's the membrana nictitans of the snakes," he mused, bethinking himself of his zoological studies. "It gives a shiny effect. But there was something more here. There was a sense of power, of wisdom—so I read them—and of weariness, utter weariness, and ineffable despair. It may be all imagination, but I never had so strong an impression. By Jove, I must have another look at them!" He rose and paced round the Egyptian rooms, but the man who had excited his curiosity had disappeared.

The student sat down again in his quiet corner and continued to work at his notes. He had gained the information which he required from the papyri, and it only remained to write it down while it was still fresh in his memory. For a time, his pencil travelled rapidly over the paper, but soon the lines became less level, the words more blurred, and finally the pencil tinkled down upon the floor, and the head of the student dropped heavily forward upon his chest.

Tired out by his journey, he slept so soundly in his lonely post behind the door that neither the clanking civil guard, nor the footsteps of sightseers, nor even the loud hoarse bell which gives the signal for closing, were sufficient to arouse him.

Twilight deepened into darkness, the bustle from the Rue de Rivoli waxed and then waned, distant Notre Dame clanged out the hour of midnight, and still the dark and lonely figure sat silently in the shadow. It was not until close upon one in the morning that, with a sudden gasp and an intaking of the breath, Vansittart Smith returned to consciousness. For a moment it flashed upon him that he had dropped asleep in his study-chair at home. The moon was shining fitfully through the unshuttered window, however, and, as his eye ran along the lines of mummies and the endless array of polished cases, he remembered clearly where he was and how he came there. The student was not a nervous man. He possessed that love of a novel situation which is peculiar to his race. Stretching out his cramped limbs, he looked at his watch and burst into a chuckle as he observed the hour. The episode would make an admirable anecdote to be introduced into his next paper as a relief to the graver and heavier speculations. He was a little cold, but wide awake and much refreshed. It was no wonder that the guardians had overlooked him, for the door threw its heavy black shadow right across him.

The complete silence was impressive. Neither outside nor inside was there a creak or a murmur. He was alone with the dead men of a dead civilisation. What though the outer city reeked of the garish nineteenth century! In all this chamber there was scarce an article, from the shrivelled ear of wheat to the pigment-box of the painter, which had not held its own against four thousand years. Here was the flotsam and jetsam washed up by the great ocean of time from that far-off empire. From stately Thebes, from lordly Luxor, from the great temples of Heliopolis, from a hundred rifled tombs, these relics had been brought. The student glanced round at the long silent figures who flickered vaguely up through the gloom, at the busy toilers who were now so restful, and he fell into a reverent and thoughtful mood. An unwonted sense of his own youth and insignificance came over him. Leaning back in his chair, he gazed dreamily down the long vista of rooms, all silvery with the moonshine, which extend through the whole wing of the widespread building. His eyes fell upon the yellow glare of a distant lamp.

John Vansittart Smith sat up on his chair with his nerves all on edge. The light was advancing slowly towards him, pausing from time to time, and then coming jerkily onwards. The bearer moved noiselessly. In the utter silence there was no suspicion of the pat of a footfall. An idea of robbers entered the Englishman's head. He snuggled up further into the corner. The light was two rooms off. Now it was in the next chamber, and still there was no sound. With something approaching to a thrill of fear the student observed a face, floating in the air as it were, behind the flare of the lamp. The figure was wrapped in shadow, but the light fell full upon the strange eager face. There was no mistaking the metallic glistening eyes and the cadaverous skin. It was the attendant with whom he had conversed.

Vansittart Smith's first impulse was to come forward and address him. A few words of explanation would set the matter clear and lead doubtless to his being conducted to some side door from which he might make his way to his hotel. As the man entered the chamber, however, there was something so stealthy in his movements, and so furtive in his expression, that the Englishman altered his intention. This was clearly no ordinary official walking the rounds. The fellow wore felt-soled slippers, stepped with a rising chest, and glanced quickly from left to right, while his hurried gasping breathing thrilled the flame of his lamp. Vansittart Smith crouched silently back into the corner and watched him keenly, convinced that his errand was one of secret and probably sinister import.

There was no hesitation in the other's movements. He stepped lightly and swiftly across to one of the great cases, and, drawing a key from his pocket, he unlocked it. From the upper shelf he pulled down a mummy, which he bore away with him, and laid it with much care and solicitude upon the ground. By it he placed his lamp, and then squatting down beside it in Eastern fashion he began with long quivering fingers to undo the cerecloths and bandages which girt it round. As the crackling rolls of linen peeled off one after the other, a strong aromatic odour filled the chamber, and fragments of scented wood and of spices pattered down upon the marble floor.

It was clear to John Vansittart Smith that this mummy had never been unswathed before. The operation interested him keenly. He thrilled all over with curiosity, and his birdlike head protruded further and further from behind the door. When, however, the last roll had been removed from the four-thousand-year-old head, it was all that he could do to stifle an outcry of amazement. First, a cascade of long, black, glossy tresses poured over the workman's hands and arms. A second turn of the bandage revealed a low, white forehead, with a pair of delicately arched eyebrows. A third uncovered a pair of bright, deeply fringed eyes, and a straight, well-cut nose, while a fourth and last showed a sweet, full, sensitive mouth, and a beautifully curved chin. The whole face was one of extraordinary loveliness, save for the one blemish that in the centre of the forehead there was a single irregular, coffee-coloured splotch. It was a triumph of the embalmer's art. Vansittart Smith's eyes grew larger and larger as he gazed upon it, and he chirruped in his throat with satisfaction.

Its effect upon the Egyptologist was as nothing, however, compared with that which it produced upon the strange attendant. He threw his hands up into the air, burst into a harsh clatter of words, and then, hurling himself down upon the ground beside the mummy, he threw his arms round her, and kissed her repeatedly upon the lips and brow. "Ma petite!" he groaned in French. "Ma pauvre petite!" His voice broke with emotion, and his innumerable wrinkles quivered and writhed, but the student observed in the lamplight that his shining eyes were still as dry and tearless as two beads of steel. For some minutes he lay, with a twitching face, crooning and moaning over the beautiful head. Then he broke into a sudden smile, said some words in an unknown tongue, and sprang to his feet with the vigorous air of one who has braced himself for an effort.

In the centre of the room there was a large circular case which contained, as the student had frequently remarked, a magnificent collection of early Egyptian rings and precious stones. To this the attendant strode, and, unlocking it, he threw it open. On the ledge at the side, he placed his lamp, and beside it a small earthenware jar which he had drawn from his pocket. He then took a handful of rings from the case, and with a most serious and anxious face he proceeded to smear each in turn with some liquid substance from the earthen pot, holding them to the light as he did so. He was clearly disappointed with the first lot, for he threw them petulantly back into the case, and drew out some more. One of these, a massive ring with a large crystal set in it, he seized and eagerly tested with the contents of the jar. Instantly he uttered a cry of joy and threw out his arms in a wild gesture which upset the pot and sent the liquid streaming across the floor to the very feet of the Englishman. The attendant drew a red handkerchief from his bosom, and, mopping up the mess, he followed it into the corner, where in a moment he found himself face to face with his observer.

"Excuse me," said John Vansittart Smith, with all imaginable politeness; "I have been unfortunate enough to fall asleep behind this door."

"And you have been watching me?" the other asked in English, with a most venomous look on his corpse-like face.

The student was a man of veracity. "I confess," said he, "that I have noticed your movements, and that they have aroused my curiosity and interest in the highest degree."

The man drew a long flamboyant-bladed knife from his bosom. "You have had a very narrow escape," he said; "had I seen you ten minutes ago, I should have driven this through your heart. As it is, if you touch me or interfere with me in any way you are a dead man."

"I have no wish to interfere with you," the student answered. "My presence here is entirely accidental. All I ask is that you will have the extreme kindness to show me out through some side door." He spoke with great suavity, for the man was still pressing the tip of his dagger against the palm of his left hand, as though to assure himself of its sharpness, while his face preserved its malignant expression.

"If I thought——" said he. "But no, perhaps it is as well. What is your name?"

The Englishman gave it.

"Vansittart Smith," the other repeated. "Are you the same Vansittart Smith who gave a paper in London upon El Kab? I saw a report of it. Your knowledge of the subject is contemptible."

"Sir!" cried the Egyptologist.

"Yet it is superior to that of many who make even greater pretensions. The whole keystone of our old life in Egypt was not the inscriptions or monuments of which you make so much, but was our hermetic philosophy and mystic knowledge, of which you say little or nothing."

"Our old life!" repeated the scholar, wide-eyed; and then suddenly, "Good God, look at the mummy's face!"

The strange man turned and flashed his light upon the dead woman, uttering a long doleful cry as he did so. The action of the air had already undone all the art of the embalmer. The skin had fallen away, the eyes had sunk inwards, the discoloured lips had writhed away from the yellow teeth, and the brown mark upon the forehead alone showed that it was indeed the same face which had shown such youth and beauty a few short minutes before.

The man flapped his hands together in grief and horror. Then mastering himself by a strong effort he turned his hard eyes once more upon the Englishman.

"It does not matter," he said, in a shaking voice. "It does not really matter. I came here to-night with the fixed determination to do something. It is now done. All else is as nothing. I have found my quest. The old curse is broken. I can rejoin her. What matter about her inanimate shell so long as her spirit is awaiting me at the other side of the veil!"

"These are wild words," said Vansittart Smith. He was becoming more and more convinced that he had to do with a madman.

"Time presses, and I must go," continued the other. "The moment is at hand for which I have waited this weary time. But I must show you out first. Come with me."

Taking up the lamp, he turned from the disordered chamber and led the student swiftly through the long series of the Egyptian, Assyrian, and Persian apartments. At the end of the latter, he pushed open a small door let into the wall and descended a winding stone stair. The Englishman felt the cold fresh air of the night upon his brow. There was a door opposite him which appeared to communicate with the street. To the right of this another door stood ajar, throwing a spurt of yellow light across the passage. "Come in here!" said the attendant shortly.

Vansittart Smith hesitated. He had hoped that he had come to the end of his adventure. Yet his curiosity was strong within him. He could not leave the matter unsolved, so he followed his strange companion into the lighted chamber.

It was a small room, such as is devoted to a concierge. A wood fire sparkled in the grate. At one side stood a truckle bed, and at the other a coarse wooden chair, with a round table in the centre, which bore the remains of a meal. As the visitor's eye glanced round, he could not but remark with an ever-recurring thrill that all the small details of the room were of the most quaint design and antique workmanship. The candlesticks, the vases upon the chimney-piece, the fire-irons, the ornaments upon the walls, were all such as he had been wont to associate with the remote past. The gnarled heavy-eyed man sat himself down upon the edge of the bed and motioned his guest into the chair.

"There may be design in this," he said, still speaking excellent English. "It may be decreed that I should leave some account behind as a warning to all rash mortals who would set their wits up against workings of Nature. I leave it with you. Make such use as you will of it. I speak to you now with my feet upon the threshold of the other world.

"I am, as you surmised, an Egyptian—not one of the down-trodden race of slaves who now inhabit the Delta of the Nile, but a survivor of that fiercer and harder people who tamed the Hebrew, drove the Ethiopian back into the southern deserts, and built those mighty works which have been the envy and the wonder of all after generations. It was in the reign of Tuthmosis, sixteen hundred years before the birth of Christ, that I first saw the light. You shrink away from me. Wait, and you will see that I am more to be pitied than to be feared.

"My name was Sosra. My father had been the chief priest of Osiris in the great temple of Abaris, which stood in those days upon the Bubastic branch of the Nile. I was brought up in the temple and was trained in all those mystic arts which are spoken of in your own Bible. I was an apt pupil. Before I was sixteen I had learned all which the wisest priest could teach me. From that time on I studied Nature's secrets for myself and shared my knowledge with no man.

"Of all the questions which attracted me there were none over which I laboured so long as over those which concern themselves with the nature of life. I probed deeply into the vital principle. The aim of medicine had been to drive away disease when it appeared. It seemed to me that a method might be devised which should so fortify the body as to prevent weakness or death from ever taking hold of it. It is useless that I should recount my researches. You would scarce comprehend them if I did. They were carried out partly upon animals, partly upon slaves, and partly on myself. Suffice it that their result was to furnish me with a substance which, when injected into the blood, would endow the body with strength to resist the effects of time, of violence, or of disease. It would not indeed confer immortality, but its potency would endure for many thousands of years. I used it upon a cat, and afterwards drugged the creature with the most deadly poisons. That cat is alive in Lower Egypt at the present moment. There was nothing of mystery or magic in the matter. It was simply a chemical discovery, which may well be made again.

"Love of life runs high in the young. It seemed to me that I had broken away from all human care now that I had abolished pain and driven death to such a distance. With a light heart I poured the accursed stuff into my veins. Then I looked round for someone whom I could benefit. There was a young priest of Thoth, Parmes by name, who had won my goodwill by his earnest nature and his devotion to his studies. To him I whispered my secret, and at his request I injected him with my elixir. I should now, I reflected, never be without a companion of the same age as myself.

"After this grand discovery I relaxed my studies to some extent, but Parmes continued his with redoubled energy. Every day I could see him working with his flasks and his distiller in the Temple of Thoth, but he said little to me as to the result of his labours. For my own part, I used to walk through the city and look around me with exultation as I reflected that all this was destined to pass away, and that only I should remain. The people would bow to me as they passed me, for the fame of my knowledge had gone abroad.

"There was war at this time, and the Great King had sent down his soldiers to the eastern boundary to drive away the Hyksos. A Governor, too, was sent to Abaris, that he might hold it for the King. I had heard much of the beauty of the daughter of this Governor, but one day as I walked out with Parmes we met her, borne upon the shoulders of her slaves. I was struck with love as with lightning. My heart went out from me. I could have thrown myself beneath the feet of her bearers. This was my woman. Life without her was impossible. I swore by the head of Horus that she should be mine. I swore it to the Priest of Thoth. He turned away from me with a brow which was as black as midnight.

"There is no need to tell you of our wooing. She came to love me even as I loved her. I learned that Parmes had seen her before I did, and had shown her that he too loved her, but I could smile at his passion, for I knew that her heart was mine. The white plague had come upon the city, and many were stricken, but I laid my hands upon the sick and nursed them without fear or scathe. She marvelled at my daring. Then I told her my secret and begged her that she would let me use my art upon her.

"'Your flower shall then be unwithered, Atma,' I said. 'Other things may pass away, but you and I, and our great love for each other, shall outlive the tomb of King Chefru.'

"But she was full of timid, maidenly objections. 'Was it right?' she asked, 'was it not a thwarting of the will of the gods? If the great Osiris had wished that our years should be so long, would he not himself have brought it about?'

"With fond and loving words, I overcame her doubts, and yet she hesitated. It was a great question, she said. She would think it over for this one night. In the morning, I should know her resolution. Surely one night was not too much to ask. She wished to pray to Isis for help in her decision.

"With a sinking heart and a sad foreboding of evil I left her with her tirewomen. In the morning, when the early sacrifice was over, I hurried to her house. A frightened slave met me upon the steps. Her mistress was ill, she said, very ill. In a frenzy I broke my way through the attendants and rushed through hall and corridor to my Atma's chamber. She lay upon her couch, her head high upon the pillow, with a pallid face and a glazed eye. On her forehead there blazed a single angry purple patch. I knew that hell-mark of old. It was the scar of the white plague, the sign-manual of death.

"Why should I speak of that terrible time? For months I was mad, fevered, delirious, and yet I could not die. Never did an Arab thirst after the sweet wells as I longed after death. Could poison or steel have shortened the thread of my existence, I should soon have rejoined my love in the land with the narrow portal. I tried, but it was of no avail. The accursed influence was too strong upon me. One night as I lay upon my couch, weak and weary, Parmes, the priest of Thoth, came to my chamber. He stood in the circle of the lamplight, and he looked down upon me with eyes which were bright with a mad joy.

"'Why did you let the maiden die?' he asked; 'why did you not strengthen her as you strengthened me?'

"'I was too late,' I answered. 'But I had forgot. You also loved her. You are my fellow in misfortune. Is it not terrible to think of the centuries which must pass ere we look upon her again? Fools, fools, that we were to take death to be our enemy!'

"'You may say that' he cried with a wild laugh; 'the words come well from your lips. For me they have no meaning.'

"'What mean you?' I cried, raising myself upon my elbow. 'Surely, friend, this grief has turned your brain.' His face was aflame with joy, and he writhed and shook like one who hath a devil.

"'Do you know whither I go?' he asked.

"'Nay,' I answered, 'I cannot tell.'

"'I go to her,' said he. 'She lies embalmed in the further tomb by the double palm-tree beyond the city wall.'

"'Why do you go there?' I asked.

"'To die!' he shrieked, 'to die! I am not bound by earthen fetters.'

"'But the elixir is in your blood,' I cried.

"'I can deny it,' said he; 'I have found a stronger principle which will destroy it. It is working in my veins at this moment, and in an hour I shall be a dead man. I shall join her, and you shall remain behind.'

"As I looked upon him I could see that he spoke words of truth. The light in his eye told me that he was indeed beyond the power of the elixir.

"'You will teach me!' I cried.

"'Never!' he answered.

"'I implore you, by the wisdom of Thoth, by the majesty of Anubis!'

"'It is useless,' he said coldly.

"'Then I will find it out,' I cried.

"'You cannot,' he answered, 'it came to me by chance. There is one ingredient which you can never get. Save that which is in the ring of Thoth, none will ever more be made.

"'In the ring of Thoth!' I repeated; 'where then is the ring of Thoth?'

"'That also you shall never know,' he answered. 'You won her love. Who has won in the end? I leave you to your sordid earth life. My chains are broken. I must go!' He turned upon his heel and fled from the chamber. In the morning came the news that the Priest of Thoth was dead.

"My days after that were spent in study. I must find this subtle poison which was strong enough to undo the elixir. From early dawn to midnight, I bent over the test-tube and the furnace. Above all, I collected the papyri and the chemical flasks of the Priest of Thoth. Alas! they taught me little. Here and there some hint or stray expression would raise hope in my bosom, but no good ever came of it. Still, month after month, I struggled on. When my heart grew faint I would make my way to the tomb by the palm-trees. There, standing by the dead casket from which the jewel had been rifled, I would feel her sweet presence, and would whisper to her that I would rejoin her if mortal wit could solve the riddle.

"Parmes had said that his discovery was connected with the ring of Thoth. I had some remembrance of the trinket. It was a large and weighty circlet, made, not of gold, but of a rarer and heavier metal brought from the mines of Mount Harbal. Platinum, you call it. The ring had, I remembered, a hollow crystal set in it, in which some few drops of liquid might be stored. Now, the secret of Parmes could not have to do with the metal alone, for there were many rings of that metal in the Temple. Was it not more likely that he had stored his precious poison within the cavity of the crystal? I had scarce come to this conclusion before, in hunting through his papers, I came upon one which told me that it was indeed so, and that there was still some of the liquid unused.

"But how to find the ring? It was not upon him when he was stripped for the embalmer. Of that I made sure. Neither was it among his private effects. In vain I searched every room that he had entered, every box, and vase, and chattel that he had owned. I sifted the very sand of the desert in the places where he had been wont to walk; but do what I would, I could come upon no traces of the ring of Thoth. Yet it may be that my labours would have overcome all obstacles had it not been for a new and unlooked-for misfortune.

"A great war had been waged against the Hyksos, and the Captains of the Great King had been cut off in the desert, with all their bowmen and horsemen. The shepherd tribes were upon us like the locusts in a dry year. From the wilderness of Shur to the great bitter lake there was blood by day and fire by night. Abaris was the bulwark of Egypt, but we could not keep the savages back. The city fell. The Governor and the soldiers were put to the sword, and I, with many more, was led away into captivity.

"For years and years, I tended cattle in the great plains by the Euphrates. My master died, and his son grew old, but I was still as far from death as ever. At last, I escaped upon a swift camel and made my way back to Egypt. The Hyksos had settled in the land which they had conquered, and their own King ruled over the country. Abaris had been torn down, the city had been burned, and of the great Temple there was nothing left save an unsightly mound. Everywhere the tombs had been rifled and the monuments destroyed. Of my Atma's grave no sign was left. It was buried in the sands of the desert, and the palm-trees which marked the spot had long disappeared. The papers of Parmes and the remains of the Temple of Thoth were either destroyed or scattered far and wide over the deserts of Syria. All search after them was vain.

"From that time, I gave up all hope of ever finding the ring or discovering the subtle drug. I set myself to live as patiently as might be until the effect of the elixir should wear away. How can you understand how terrible a thing time is, you who have experience only of the narrow course which lies between the cradle and the grave! I know it to my cost, I who have floated down the whole stream of history. I was old when Ilium fell. I was very old when Herodotus came to Memphis. I was bowed down with years when the new gospel came upon earth. Yet you see me much as other men are, with the cursed elixir still sweetening my blood, and guarding me against that which I would court. Now at last, at last I have come to the end of it!

"I have travelled in all lands, and I have dwelt with all nations. Every tongue is the same to me. I learned them all to help pass the weary time. I need not tell you how slowly they drifted by, the long dawn of modern civilisation, the dreary middle years, the dark times of barbarism. They are all behind me now, I have never looked with the eyes of love upon another woman. Atma knows that I have been constant to her.

"It was my custom to read all that the scholars had to say upon Ancient Egypt. I have been in many positions, sometimes affluent, sometimes poor, but I have always found enough to enable me to buy the journals which deal with such matters. Some nine months ago I was in San Francisco, when I read an account of some discoveries made in the neighbourhood of Abaris. My heart leapt into my mouth as I read it. It said that the excavator had busied himself in exploring some tombs recently unearthed. In one there had been found an unopened mummy with an inscription upon the outer case setting forth that it contained the body of the daughter of the Governor of the city in the days of Tuthmosis. It added that on removing the outer case there had been exposed a large platinum ring set with a crystal, which had been laid upon the breast of the embalmed woman. This, then was where Parmes had hid the ring of Thoth. He might well say that it was safe, for no Egyptian would ever stain his soul by moving even the outer case of a buried friend.

"That very night I set off from San Francisco, and in a few weeks I found myself once more at Abaris, if a few sand-heaps and crumbling walls may retain the name of the great city. I hurried to the Frenchmen who were digging there and asked them for the ring. They replied that both the ring and the mummy had been sent to the Boulak Museum at Cairo. To Boulak I went, but only to be told that Mariette Bey had claimed them and had shipped them to the Louvre. I followed them, and there at last, in the Egyptian chamber, I came, after close upon four thousand years, upon the remains of my Atma, and upon the ring for which I had sought so long.

"But how was I to lay hands upon them? How was I to have them for my very own? It chanced that the office of attendant was vacant. I went to the Director. I convinced him that I knew much about Egypt. In my eagerness I said too much. He remarked that a Professor's chair would suit me better than a seat in the Conciergerie. I knew more, he said, than he did. It was only by blundering and letting him think that he had over-estimated my knowledge, that I prevailed upon him to let me move the few effects which I have retained into this chamber. It is my first and my last night here.

"Such is my story, Mr. Vansittart Smith. I need not say more to a man of your perception. By a strange chance you have this night looked upon the face of the woman whom I loved in those far-off days. There were many rings with crystals in the case, and I had to test for the platinum to be sure of the one which I wanted. A glance at the crystal has shown me that the liquid is indeed within it, and that I shall at last be able to shake off that accursed health which has been worse to me than the foulest disease. I have nothing more to say to you. I have unburdened myself. You may tell my story, or you may withhold it at your pleasure. The choice rests with you. I owe you some amends, for you have had a narrow escape of your life this night. I was a desperate man, and not to be baulked in my purpose. Had I seen you before the thing was done, I might have put it beyond your power to oppose me or to raise an alarm. This is the door. It leads into the Rue de Rivoli. Good night!"

The Englishman glanced back. For a moment the lean figure of Sosra the Egyptian stood framed in the narrow doorway. The next the door had slammed, and the heavy rasping of a bolt broke on the silent night.

It was on the second day after his return to London that Mr. John Vansittart Smith saw the following concise narrative in the Paris correspondence of the Times:—

"Curious Occurrence in the Louvre.—Yesterday morning a strange discovery was made in the principal Egyptian Chamber. The ouvriers who are employed to clean out the rooms in the morning found one of the attendants lying dead upon the floor with his arms round one of the mummies. So close was his embrace that it was only with the utmost difficulty that they were separated. One of the cases containing valuable rings had been opened and rifled. The authorities are of opinion that the man was bearing away the mummy with some idea of selling it to a private collector, but that he was struck down in the very act by long-standing disease of the heart. It is said that he was a man of uncertain age and eccentric habits, without any living relations to mourn over his dramatic and untimely end."

THE END